I0747214

and the multiple, and above all between the stagger-
ingly alien and the cosily familiar. A cleverly executed
balance of heartbreak and hope."

—J. S. Breukelaar, Aurealis and Shirley Jackson Award
finalist for *Aletheia* and *Collision:Stories*

"Inventive, clever, and pleasingly Cronenbergesque."

— Priya Sharma, Shirley Jackson Award and British
Fantasy Award winning author of *All the Fabulous
Beasts*

"*Zoi* is a new and refreshing take on first contact stories as well as the idea and role of the doppelgänger. It
is a quietly philosophical book about choices and determination that follows the narrator, Amira, on her
journey of transformation and adaptation. With its
diverse cast and contemporary views, I am tempted to
call *Zoi* a modern *Solaris*, but it is an original novel that
stands fully on its own. I found myself deeply invested
in the book and would recommend it to fans of Sue
Burke and Becky Chambers, and everybody else who
enjoys science fiction that is both solid and approach-
able."

— Marie Howalt, author of the *Moonless* Trilogy, *Colibri
Investigations* and *A Study in Black Brew*

Also by Jane Mondrup

Vattes Vandring (Danish, 2024, Superlux)
Zeitgeist (Danish, 2019, Vandkunsten)

Learn more at janemondrup.dk

ZOI

A NOVEL

JANE MONDRUP

Denver, Colorado

Published in the United States by:
Spaceboy Books LLC
1627 Vine Street
Denver, CO 80206
www.readspaceboy.com

ISBN: 978-1-951393-42-7
First printed June 2025

For my mother and my daughter.

We are all subjects to biology in strange and sometimes unfair ways. Being born or giving birth. Growing up or growing old. This is a book about strangeness, connection, and love. I love you both.

CHANGES

The hologram zooms in on Natan. Throughout the recording, he has been updating me on his own life and what's going on in his family. I know him well enough to sense the concern beneath the cheerful tone. Now it surfaces, both in his face and his voice.

"That's all for now. But I hope to hear from you soon. Of course, I understand if it's difficult to find the time, or the energy. You're in a pretty extreme situation."

One of the child voices I've been hearing in the background rises to a squeal. An adult shushes them. Natan continues:

"Maybe you don't want to deal with anything coming from Earth. But I'd be grateful to get a holo from you once in a while, no matter what it contains."

He's right. It's painful enough to watch this

depiction of him, hear it talk about a world I'll never see again. The message had been waiting for me for several days before I finally worked up the courage to open it. Sending a reply seems insurmountable. It's been at least a month since I last did it. Possibly longer.

"I know through ETLEA that you're still alive, or that you were when you last sent a status report. That just doesn't tell me how you're doing. What you're experiencing. What you're thinking."

It was easier when we could still speak directly, that is, as directly as the distance of a few light minutes allows. During previous expeditions we had gotten used to the inbuilt pauses. It was like talking to a very thoughtful person who carefully considered all their answers before speaking, but it still felt like a conversation. When the zoi broke out of its orbit, we continued like that until the pauses got too long, and we had to give up. Since then, our communication has consisted of holorecordings going back and forth, and you can always postpone those. Besides, I don't know what to say.

"No pressure. I'll keep sending messages no matter how often you answer. As long as I do that, I haven't lost you completely." He raises his hand in farewell. "Goodbye for now, Amira. Take care and give my best to the others."

The recording ends. Natan's figure disappears, leaving me alone in the holoroom. I hang in midair while arguing with myself. Of course, I ought to make a recording right away. Natan stressed that it doesn't matter what it contains. I don't have to give a full account of all current events. Not that it would be much of an ordeal, considering how little is actually happening. But then, what can I tell him? How I feel? What I'm thinking? I hardly know that myself.

Around me, I see the zoi organelles, large and small, move around in the cytosol fluid, delimited from the air in the room by a partly transparent membrane. Sometimes, I still catch myself thinking that they are watching me. By now, we're pretty sure they're just cell components without any agency or self-awareness. They're not independent beings. But they look like that.

It ought to be an inexhaustible subject: the zoi itself. The fact that I reside within a living creature, a denizen of open space, one that travels from one star to another. It's a form of travel that used to reside within the realm of fantasy, and no matter how uneventful it appears, it's an adventure. On this journey, we're truly getting to know this alien being, the zoi. Though we're not doing much about it right now. At least, I'm not.

Minutes pass. My arms float in front of me, as they do in zero g when you let them. Once or twice, I make a halfhearted gesture towards the recorder, but that's all it comes to.

Finally, I give up.

I close the transparent cover shielding the holo projector from the zoi environment, and a slight kick against the wall membrane propels me towards the exit. The simple act of opening and closing the door makes me think of Linn. While the rooms and the passages connecting them are created by the zoi, the mechanisms closing off some of the rooms were developed by Linn during the previous expedition.

Linn's special skills are among the primary reasons this journey could even be considered. She's an expert in BB-tech, biology-based technology, and her most important task is to manipulate various zoi substances to develop the right properties, suited for technology components and utility items. But she hasn't been able to work for a long time. In fact, she has felt ill throughout both this and the previous expedition, but she managed to conceal it, until it was too late.

I continue down the passageway, past Linn's quarters which are located next to the holoroom. The transmitter on my arm is buzzing, reminding me that it's almost three o'clock. It's a primitive model, not even able to generate holograms, but it can withstand the humid air and the changing chemical effects from the surroundings. The zoi has created an environment that accommodates human needs, but only extended to our biology. Technology must fend for itself, and our equipment is always in danger of being dissolved and absorbed as nourishment. That's why most of it is shielded behind protective surfaces while we're not using it. The transmitters are the only things we carry around with us.

Now at least I know what to do with myself. With deliberate kicks and pushes I move through the passageway in the direction of the living room for my daily meetup with the other three. From the beginning Evardo insisted on making it a regular appointment, and though I would sometimes rather be excused, it's something to hold on to. I need that right now.

The living room is the largest air-filled space in the zoi, located centrally in the network of air pockets and passageways constituting our home. It was here the first air bubbles emerged, beginning the now familiar process that I have personally experienced three times.

Evardo and Linn are waiting inside. I notice how thin Linn has become. Dark shadows have established themselves permanently under her eyes, and her round cheeks have sunk in. Her Scandinavian skin is inherently pale, but it has acquired an unhealthy, yellowish hue. She may have started losing hair. It isn't clear because she keeps it short, but I think I spot her scalp in several places. Besides, I have suspiciously often come across short, fair hair straws floating in the air in places where Linn has been.

She looks old, and she is only thirty-one, the youngest of us by far. At the departure she was in superior shape. We were all training hard, but as always, she made an extra effort. Maybe it has helped her a little, but not enough.

"Hello, Amira."

It's Evardo, formal and quiet as always. He's the oldest in the crew, forty-seven as far as I remember. Evardo has been my doctor for twelve years, ever since I got enlisted as an astronaut at Extra Terrestrial Life Exploration Agency, in short ETLEA. Back then no one would have imagined that the earthbound physician would even consider personally joining a space mission. But he surprised us all.

I mutter a greeting to them both. Linn smiles back faintly, takes a deep breath, and exhales slowly.

I gently stroke her arm. "One of the worse days, right?"

"Yes." Her voice is weak but steadies somewhat when she continues: "I feel miserable. It's like something's happening to me. Evardo tries to figure out what it is, but I don't think he's getting any wiser."

Evardo clears his throat. "May I take a blood sample from you, Amira?"

"From me? Why?"

"Because I just took one from myself, and the analysis showed some interesting results. But first tell me: how are you feeling?"

I hesitate. I don't feel all that well, but I figured it was psychological.

"Not sure," I answer. "Maybe a bit weird."

"Then let's see what the blood sample says."

Obediently, I extend a hand. Evardo pricks my finger with a little instrument that also does the analysis. He nods to himself.

"It matches mine in showing distinct hormonal changes compared to the last sample. On the other hand, there's no sign of infection."

"Infection?" I give him a puzzled look. "You never get infections in a zoi."

"It hasn't happened yet," he concedes, "which is no guarantee, but it doesn't seem to be the explanation in this case. It's hormones, once again."

Evardo glances at Linn who is fidgeting uneasily. Hormone levels racing up and down is the source of her health problems. We're all subject to hormonal stimuli from the zoi, but Linn's immune defense system seems to be especially hostile to the external influence. Her adverse reactions cause the zoi to continually modify those stimuli, which makes her system go into even higher alert.

It started out like that for all of us, both on this expedition and the previous ones. Kiah has compared it to being pregnant. She's the only one of us who has had that experience, and according to her, it felt somewhat similar: nausea, coupled with a constant restlessness making it almost impossible to sleep or even relax, no matter how tired she was. For the rest of us, these ailments eventually subsided. But Linn has only gotten worse.

When I first met Linn, I felt a certain aversion towards her, perhaps because she seemed like a more successful version of myself. But all envy is gone now. I still don't know Linn that well, as she has always been reserved. But I feel sorry for her. I know how wretched she must feel, and I expect that by now, she has given up hope that it will ever pass.

Are we all heading for the same misery? The thought worsens my slight nausea.

"What about Kiah?" I ask. "Have you taken a blood sample from her?"

"Not yet." Evardo looks towards the passageway leading to Kiah's quarters.

I tap on the transmitter. It's long past three o'clock. A grumpy remark escapes me:

"I'm getting tired of waiting for her."

Evardo regards me with mild disapproval. "She isn't always late," he points out. "Sometimes she turns up long before the rest of us."

Both his tone of voice and his gaze reminds me of my father. It only adds to my annoyance.

"Well, yes. But if only she let her transmitter give a reminder, she could be on time. It would be easier for all of us."

"Amira, we each have our way of settling into the situation. Kiah feels more comfortable without the transmitter. We have to respect that."

I suppose we do. We can't afford to argue over trifles like that. A positive atmosphere between the crew members must be maintained at all costs. But the little things are adding up, setting Kiah apart from the rest of us. She and I used to be friends. We started at ETLEA around the same time, and we both joined the two zoi expeditions prior to this one. Now, I feel like I don't know her anymore.

A couple more minutes pass, then she floats into the living room, naked as always. That in itself doesn't bother me. We were never shy around each other, and I have seen her athletic, brown body lots of times, both back on earth and during previous expeditions. The problem is what her nakedness represents: Kiah's quick and efficient adaptation to the environment. She feels just peachy in the zoi, physically and mentally. In return, she's uncomfortable with some of the stuff we have brought from Earth, such as clothes.

She approaches us without any greeting, without any word at all. Her gaze seems distant, as if she's thinking of something more important than us.

"Kiah, I would like to take a blood sample," Evardo says. "There's something we need to investigate."

Not asking any questions, Kiah extends a finger

for Evardo to prick. Then she becomes a bit more attentive. She focuses on Evardo while he reads the results of the blood analysis.

"What does it say?" She sounds both curious and detached. Right now, she's focused on us, but she may lose interest at any moment.

"More or less what I expected: significant fluctuations in your hormonal levels, similar to the test results for the rest of us. Have you noticed any changes yourself, either in your physical condition or your mood?"

"Changes?" Once again Kiah's gaze goes on long distance. "Yes. Something is happening. I feel... not tired, but as if I need to be left alone."

Those words make my blood pressure grow. Need to be left alone! We leave Kiah to herself almost all the time. She hardly ever seeks us out, except for the daily meetings, and if you manage to talk to her, all you get is a bunch of nonsense, as if she operates on an entirely different logic than the rest of us.

"Well, then we should probably leave you in peace," I state coolly. "You don't have to stay any longer if our company tires you."

"Amira." It's Evardo with another fatherly reproach. "Kiah was just answering my question. She can't control how she feels."

"No, and neither can I!"

I want to let it all out—my anger, my loneliness, my fear of both tangible and undefined threats. But

Evardo's gaze stops me.

"Your feelings are probably amplified by the hormonal changes we have detected. They throw us all out of balance."

"Even you?"

Evardo ignores my sarcastic tone. "Yes, even me. And I know that if I say exactly what I want to, I will probably regret it later. For that reason, I suggest we end the meeting. If any of you find your condition worsening, please call on me. But for now, I think we should all go our separate ways."

So, we do.

When my temper has settled somewhat, it's a relief. I also need peace and quiet. Even though I feel lonely, I can't cope with any kind of company. For the rest of the day, I keep to myself, and when the bioluminescence starts to turn down in the early evening, I retreat to my bedchamber.

Though I've hardly lifted a finger today, I'm overwhelmingly tired. Something inside me is at work, and I'm too exhausted to wonder what.

OBSERVATION

When the first zoi appeared, I was five years old; too young to truly understand the meaning of the pictures that Uncle Karim showed me in holo format, but old enough to be captivated by the sight of the shining lump between the stars. Fluctuating patterns of color ran across the surface as the lump slowly changed shape.

I sat on Karim's lap, watching the hologram.

"Why is it bulging?" I asked. "Did it eat too much?"

"You may say it's getting ready to eat. Or to absorb energy, in the form of light from the sun. When it traveled through space, it made sense for it to be oblong, so it didn't collide with as much other stuff. Now that it has gone into orbit, it's widening its shape, and the area facing the sun darkens in order to absorb more light. Look."

Karim switched to another recording. Here, the lump first looked like a ball, but it rotated before my eyes; not all the way around, but enough that I could see it had flattened, and that the other side was almost black. Not completely, for the dark surface still had a play of colors, with faint traces of light dancing across. I watched them, filled with wonder and excitement, partly because I sensed the same from Karim.

I loved Karim. He was my mother's little brother, much younger than her, and he was different from all other grownups. Not only because he was young. I had teenage cousins who were just as boring as my parents. But Karim always had interesting things to show or tell me about. Far off places he wanted to visit someday. People doing exciting stuff like building new communities in places ravaged by climate disasters, diving to the bottom of the sea to explore the ecosystem down there or studying the vast night space around the Earth.

"Is it some kind of animal?" I asked.

"Possibly. The scientists are pretty sure it's alive."

"It looks friendly. Do you think I could visit it?"

Karim looked down at me. "Maybe someday," he said smilingly. "Who knows?"

The astronomers had spotted the elongated shape as it passed by Earth. It didn't look like anything they had seen before, so they followed it closely, discovering that it changed shape, decelerated and altered its course to orbit the sun. None of those things would happen of their own accord.

At first, most people believed that it was a spaceship. The course change looked like a deliberate maneuver, and the shape was emitting radio waves which might be an attempt at communication. But these waves quickly turned out to be too unvaried to contain any messages. Since the shape entered its orbit around the sun, located halfway between Earth and the planet called Venus, the signals had stopped. The object showed no other sign of activity or of having anyone on board. All investigation confirmed the impression that this wasn't a vehicle, but something that was itself alive.

For the next two years, we followed the studies of the large creature, which was first named *zoion*, a word meaning *living being* in some old language, but it was quickly shortened to *zoi*. Gradually, I built up some understanding of the relation between Earth, the solar system and the universe. Earth was only one among countless planets, and the stars were suns like our own, incredibly far away. No planet in our solar system, apart from the Earth, had turned out to be habitable, so we had never met any other form of life.

But now, the zoi had arrived out of the immense emptiness between our solar system and all the others. Life on Earth had company.

Not everyone liked that idea. Many initially feared that the zoi would attack us, or that someone inside it would do so. Despite being alive, the zoi could still have passengers. It may be populated by intelligent beings who had destroyed their planet and now were searching for a new one. That scenario seemed quite likely, considering how humanity itself had behaved. We had come close to destroying Earth.

But nothing indicated that the zoi or anyone inside it had ill intensions. A number of unmanned probes were launched, keeping a respectful distance at first. The zoi never reacted to their presence, not even when they got close. The astronomers now hazarded a direct examination of the surface, still prompting no reaction from the zoi, but also yielding no results. The smooth, impenetrable shell rejected all attempts to scrape or drill. It also turned out impossible to transilluminate, no matter which technique was used.

Just under two years after the zoi's arrival it began to change shape and color again. The dark surface grew lighter while the flattened shape first swelled into a sphere and then began to stretch itself long. At the same time, it accelerated and broke out of orbit. A brief panic ensued when, for a while, it looked like it was headed for Earth, but once again it passed at a safe distance and continued towards the outer reaches of the solar system.

Karim and I closely followed the zoi's departure. A probe was sent after it, but it never caught up with the zoi, which accelerated through space, faster and faster, driven by forces unknown to the scientists. Day by day, observations of it got dimmer as the distance increased.

I cried when I saw the last speck of light vanish. For two years, the zoi had been there as a huge, silent friend, and then it just disappeared.

"Why did it leave us?" I asked Karim. "We never got to talk to it, and now it's gone."

"Amira, it probably wasn't the kind of being you can talk to. It showed no signs of intelligence. If it was intelligent, it evidently wasn't interested in us."

"Maybe it was hurt because we never came up to see it," I said, tears streaming down my face. "It waited so long for us, and we just sent those probe robots. It must have thought we didn't like it."

Karim stroked my hair. "It's not that simple. Human space travel is very expensive, and it takes a long time to organize. We have been following the preparations. It would have taken years to get ready."

"Well, then they should have started earlier," I declared with all the conviction of a seven-year-old. "And they should have hurried. Now it's too late!" I looked angrily at Karim, as if it was his fault, which, in a way, I felt it was. He was a grownup. He could have done something.

Karim knew better than to argue. He stood up, went to the window and looked at the darkening sky. The first stars were blinking into existence on the dark blue background.

"Yes, it's too late for now, but not necessarily forever. Maybe we will get another chance."

"You think so?" I wiped away my tears.

"Why not? If it happened once, it can happen again. Another zoi may show up, or some completely different kind of creature."

"I hope it will be a zoi. It seemed so kind, even though it didn't say anything."

I leaned against him, and he wrapped his arm around me.

"I think so too," he said.

We stood there for a moment, then I pulled free and climbed into the windowsill.

"If another zoi comes by when I'm grown, I will go up to visit it. Just try to stop me!"

"I have no intention of doing so."

Karim sounded amused. I glared at him.

"Don't laugh at me."

His crooked smile vanished, and he shook his head gravely.

"I'm not laughing. I may have been smiling a little, because you seem so determined. But it's good to be determined, especially when it comes to choosing your own path in life."

His eyes darted towards the door separating his room from the rest of the house. I thought about the discussions I had overheard between Karim and my grandparents, sometimes also my mother, about what he should do after finishing some level of education. They wanted him to keep studying, but he didn't want to. I knew he was twenty-one years old, and I could fully understand if he was tired of schools by now and would like to do something else. Karim wanted to travel and help people around the world with all kinds of things. To me, that sounded very sensible.

"I believe you, Amira," he continued. "You will go to space, if you really want to."

"And meet a zoi?" I asked.

"Yes, if more of them are out there. Let's hope they are."

SHADOWS

'm still tired when I wake up, even though I've slept heavily all night. Whatever is happening in my body, it's still ongoing. It's not as bad as during the adaptation phase, but I feel sluggish and queasy, and I lack the energy to move or interact with anyone. Instead of getting up, I stay in my bedchamber. Usually, I wouldn't linger there during the day, but right now, I feel like hiding.

Basically, my private living space consists of a single, smallish cave with pliable walls, well suited for sleeping because you can't float around too much or bump into anything hard. The wall membrane is completely opaque; something which in this case happened by itself, perhaps because the zoi registered how visual stimuli can disturb our sleep. In other areas we have intentionally altered the opacity to suit the room's function, using methods Linn has developed.

Opposite the entrance, my few personal belongings are huddled together behind an organic grid. Linn helped me make it while we were still in orbit. Now, some of the strings have gone slack, and the smallest objects tend to work their way out and float around the room. But I'm even too weary to do anything about that.

Of course, I can't stay in here forever. I'm getting hungry, and I have almost emptied the water tube I keep inside the grid. Sooner or later, I will also need to use the toilet.

Eventually, I pull myself together. I move through the entrance and continue down the passageways, towards the room designed for disposing of bodily waste. To my relief, it's vacant, so I lock myself in, prepare the toilet seat and turn on the vacuum tube. The tube is technology we brought with us; employing the same basic principle that space shuttles and stations always relied on. Suction does gravity's work, ensuring that the waste does not end up floating around in the air. But from that point, the zoi takes care of it.

It happens on the other side of the lavatory's wall membrane, in a bubble outside the habitat, our air-filled territory. An analysis of samples from the latrine bubble conveyed that our waste products are being converted into a substance which we aren't yet sure if the zoi can consume directly or needs to process further. Transporter organelles move between the latrine bubble and the nutrient deposits we call vacuoles. They don't correspond exactly to vacuoles in earthly cells, but they are similar enough to go by the same name. The vacuoles form a complex system of variously sized containers. So far, we have a limited understanding of how they function, both on their own and as a part of the larger organism.

Sitting on the toilet seat, I pull a couple of cloths from the net fastened to the nearby wall. The seat provides a gentle rinse, but it's important to wipe thoroughly afterwards. The cloths are made from zoi material, a spongy substance suited for absorbing liquid. With another cloth, moistened with water from a tube, I wash my hands. I throw all cloths in the toilet before turning it off and conclude by disinfecting my hands in a similarly zoi-based gel.

The zoi provides us with air, water and food, and we can make a number of other necessities from its substances. But not all. The toilet seat and vacuum tubes are examples of devices we are nowhere near being able to reproduce. We have a certain stock of spare parts, but according to plan we should be well on our way to manufacturing them ourselves at this point.

Almost all the technology we brought is made of organic materials, and in principle, it should be possible to fabricate both components and entirely new devices out of materials synthesized from zoi substances. Unfortunately, we haven't made nearly as much progress in this field as we had counted on. We placed our trust in Linn, as the rest of us have a very limited understanding of BB-tech. With my xenobiology expertise, I ought to be the best qualified for taking over Linn's work, but when she tries to explain the engineering side of it to me, I have a hard time following her. Besides, I lack the manual dexterity which is just as important as theory.

Kiah has that dexterity. Though her professional expertise lies within psychology and communication, she seems to have an inherent feel for the zoi substances, and she can more or less mold them as the wants. But the technological aspect is beyond her abilities, and maybe also interests. To me, she seems unnecessarily dismissive of acquainting herself with it. Perhaps she sees it as disturbing her perfect adaptation to the zoi.

After leaving the lavatory, I move towards the living room, which is the hub of all passageways, and from there I continue towards the pantry; the spot where nutrients can be plucked from the wall, and water reserves are available behind a thin membrane.

By now I'm famished, and at the same time I feel nauseous. Eating the food that the zoi produces for us is never particularly enjoyable, and right now the mere thought is downright repulsive. But my hunger and nausea seem to amplify each other, and I need to get something in my stomach. I force down a few lumps of the stuff, and I feel a little better. My urgent physical needs have been satisfied. For the first time today, I'm able to think beyond them.

I look around and listen down the passageway. It seems a little strange that I haven't run into anyone, especially Evardo. The fact that he hasn't been around to check on the rest of us is rather worrying. I'd better go and find him.

The way to Evardo's quarters takes me through the living room. Just as I glide through the opening between the passageway and the large room, I notice it.

The shadow.

It may have been there for some time without me discovering it, as it's barely visible. My eyes have probably registered it as one of the many cell components swimming around me. But it's not in the cytosol, on the other side of the membrane. It's here, inside the air-filled passageway, right beside me. It sticks to me.

"Amira?"

Linn's voice comes from the passageway leading to her bedchamber and the holoroom. It sounds weak, but also tinged with panic. She enters the living room with a skewed kick that propels her through the air, spinning and at too high a pace. She's headed straight for me. I raise my hands to cushion the impact.

Before she hits me, I catch a glimpse of a faint silhouette following the outline of her body. Then we collide, and my hand brushes against something soft and sticky. Her shadow.

Linn's eyes flicker between the two elongated masses of clearly biological material; the one next to her and the one next to me.

"So... you have one too."

I nod. Out of the corner of my eye, I see the shadow following even this small movement, just as an optical shadow would, but there are no optical shadows in the zoi, as bioluminescence illuminates us from all angles. I haven't seen a regular shadow for nearly two years.

"What is it?" Linn asks in a trembling voice. She looks sideways, towards the shadow. Slowly she raises her hand, as if to touch the jellyfish-like substance, but then she halts the movement. A shiver runs through her, and she turns her head away.

"I have no idea." I reach for my own shadow. Even though I use the opposite hand, some part of it still moves—perhaps the vestige of an arm, with narrow strings going through the transparent material, suggesting the shape of a hand. The all but invisible shadow fingers flutter in the air while I touch the more substantial part, next to my upper body. The tacky surface yields to even the slightest touch. Instinctively, I pull my hand back, afraid that the touch might cause harm or even pain to the thing that seems almost like a part of me.

"It's alive," Linn exclaims with terror in her

voice. "And it's stuck on me. I can't get it off!"

Linn has reached the limit of what she can handle calmly and with composure. I'm still able to keep my reaction under control, mainly for her sake.

"It must be made by the zoi," I say. "And the zoi means us no harm. It does its best to satisfy our needs."

"Perhaps it means us no harm," Linn grits out, "but it is harming *me*. It makes me ill. And now this happens."

What can I say? Fortunately, Evardo floats in from one of the passageways, just at that moment. He too has a companion; an oblong blob at his side, akin to ours. From a distance it's even more apparent how it follows the contours of our bodies. It's slimmer, but where the body is broadest, it is too. Up by the head, it seems to have extra substance. Here, the material looks more solid; at least it's less transparent. The same goes for some lumps farther down, which could well represent internal organs.

The heart is easiest to identify. It's just a lump of somewhat darker and firmer material, but I can see it beating vaguely, though I wonder what it's pumping. The lines connected to it are too pale and faint to contain blood. It's all just rudimentary formations. In most cases, only their location discloses what they represent. Two murky patches around the heart must be the lungs. Other colorations can be seen where the liver and kidney would be. The darkened spots are interlinked by lines, most distinguishable between the head and the torso, while weaker traces extend to the extremities. Blood vessels, maybe nerve pathways too.

None of us say anything until Evardo has caught up with us.

"When did you discover them?" he asks in his judicious doctor's voice. If he is frightened, he's hiding it well.

"I've only just noticed mine," I reply.

Evardo shifts his gaze to Linn.

"I don't know." Her voice is little more than a whisper, and she speaks too quickly, as if she wants it over with. "At first, I thought it was a dream. I've hardly slept, and I... wasn't sure if I had fallen asleep. If I was seeing things. But then I could feel it, sticking to me."

Linn tightens her lips and closes her eyes. Drops of sweat are forming on her brow, and she's even paler than usual. Is she about to faint? I glance at Evardo.

"Linn." He puts a hand on her shoulder. She inhales in a gasp, and her eyes widen. Evardo addresses her again, in a calm and insistent voice. "Your reaction is understandable. You're already exhausted, and this is a shock. I still haven't figured out what kind of phenomenon we're experiencing, but nothing indicates that it's dangerous. I will try to examine it, and then we'll discuss it. Right now, I think you should try to get some sleep."

"I don't want to be alone!"

Bubbles float into the air from Linn's eyes. I hate crying in zero g myself. Instead of running down your cheeks, the tears collect into a screen in front of your eyes, making you nearly blind. Linn doesn't seem to care. Either she is too exhausted, or she has become used to weightless tears. I've only seen her cry a few times, but who knows what she does when she's alone?

"Then stay here with us. But take a break."

Linn's shoulders tremble, her tears are followed by a resigned sobbing. Slowly it fades, and her body begins to relax.

"I'll look after you," Evardo continues. "Just sleep."

Gradually, Linn's breathing becomes slow and steady. She hovers in the air, her arms floating in front of her. Her shadow also remains still. Evardo watches it with a slight frown.

"What do you think it is?" I ask quietly.

"I'd rather reserve judgment until we know a little more, such as whether all four of us have them. Will you find Kiah? I'll stay here with Linn."

I nod and make my way towards the passageway leading to Kiah's quarters. Not that I have any desire to seek her out, but Evardo has a point. Right now, we need all the information we can get.

INVITATION

I was eleven years old when the second zoi arrived in our solar system. It was discovered much earlier than the first, as the astronomers were keeping an eye out for radio waves of the same frequency as those emitted by the first zoi. Up to a point, this signal had enabled the astronomers to track the alien creature as it left the solar system. In the Kuiper Belt the signal got weaker and then completely disappeared.

A few years later, they picked up a similar signal coming from an object heading towards the solar system at an oblique angle. Instead of going straight through, it changed its course when it reached the system's disk in the asteroid belt between Mars and Jupiter and started to move along it in the direction of the sun. Space telescope observations soon confirmed it to be another zoi.

I followed this second arrival on my own. Karim was in Bangladesh, participating in an effort to restore regions devastated by floods, making them habitable again. He rarely had internet access, which was almost unfathomable to me. Instead of speaking directly, we exchanged text and video messages, and I was the one who had to keep him updated on current events.

No one else understood my fascination with the zois. The idea of alien life did appeal to a few of my classmates, but they quickly grew tired of hearing about it. After all, nothing much had happened last time. The zoi might be an extraterrestrial, but it was a boring one; just a big lump of something which was supposedly alive. Not much of a phenomenon for the average child.

My parents approved of my interest in science, but they didn't have the time or inclination to delve into the subject with me. I would watch extensive VR recordings on my own, read articles that I hardly understood at first, and when the first steps towards the formation of ETLEA were taken—even before the second zoi had passed Earth and settled into roughly the same orbit as its predecessor—I eagerly followed along.

The Extra Terrestrial Life Exploration Agency started as a collaboration between existing space agencies, various universities, and institutions on state and supranational levels, but the need for swift action soon transformed it into an independent organization. The first zoi had orbited the sun for less than two years, and we couldn't expect its successor to stay any longer.

Space exploration hadn't been particularly high on the priority list in the preceding decades, characterized as they were by climate catastrophes and rebuilding efforts. A couple of manned expeditions to Mars in the middle of the century had been enormously costly, and the results had not justified the effort. Keeping humans alive in space or on a foreign planet was in short term unreasonably resource-intensive and probably impossible in the long run. In an age with plenty of problems to tackle, it seemed wrong to spend too much energy on such endeavors.

That didn't mean space research was abandoned. A number of stations were kept in orbit around Earth and used for various scientific purposes. New and improved space telescopes were regularly launched, to gather astronomical data in general, and especially to monitor space-derived threats, such as asteroids and solar storms. Unmanned probes were sent to a growing number of bodies in the solar system. If humanity's dream of populating space wasn't exactly dead, it at least lay dormant. Only a few romantics still believed it would ever happen.

The discovery of the zoi had briefly created an atmosphere of sensation, fueled by the fear of invasion as well as hope that the galaxy would now open to us. When none of that came to pass, public interest dwindled and only partly revived when another zoi appeared. Only scientists fully grasped the importance of encountering a non-Earthly life form, regardless of whether it was intelligent or not. Many fundamental questions about the origin, distribution and diversity of life could finally be answered. We had missed the first opportunity. This time we had to seize it.

But what would that entail? In some papers I read, the authors argued for capturing the zoi and bringing it to Earth—not down to the planet, for even the most ruthless would recognize that a creature adapted to life in empty space couldn't survive the gravity here—but into an orbit from where we could study it at our leisure. Sooner or later, we would find a way to penetrate the surface and see what was inside.

To my immense relief, there were too many arguments against that suggestion. Not only the one obvious to me: that it would be an outrageous assault against a being that had done nothing to harm us; but also that it was too risky. The zoi was massive. In the spherical shape, which was the intermediary stage between its elongated travel form and the flattened shape suited for absorbing sunlight, it was about twenty meters in diameter. The unexplained forces driving it through space might conceivably be weaponized. Any aggressive move on our part could have immeasurable consequences, possibly for all of humanity.

Instead, the goal became a manned expedition, sent to study the zoi before it took off again. It was barely possible within the time frame we had, if this zoi stayed for the same duration as the first one.

When the manned expedition was sent off, I stayed up all night with Karim who was home for a while. Before the transmission began, I heard him arguing with my mother. She wanted me to stick to my bedtime, so I would be well rested for school next day. Karim presented a few counterarguments, but he mostly ignored her. The two of us were going to watch that launch, no matter what she thought about it.

A couple of weeks later, when the expedition arrived at the zoi, we were glued to the VR for hours on end, following every broadcasted second of the first encounter.

One of the astronauts donned a spacesuit to close the remaining gap between the shuttle and the alien being. Not that anyone expected he would achieve much by doing so, but the act carried symbolic weight. Two living creatures meeting in empty space.

Through the astronaut's camera we observed the

shimmering colors on the zoi's surface. They made it look inviting, however hard and repellent it had turned out to be. I wanted to reach out and touch it, and I saw the astronaut extend his hand to place it on the surface.

He held it there for a few seconds. Then he jerked back and shouted something which I later learned meant *what the fuck* in Korean. The surface gave way to his touch. It was sucked inwards, leaving a cavity fit for the size of a human body.

An airlock.

Agitated cries went back and forth between the astronaut and his crewmates in the shuttle. This was an invitation. I held my breath while they debated what he should do. He seemed to consider following the zoi's silent suggestion and enter the airlock, but the others talked him out of it.

The astronauts stayed with the zoi for two weeks, examining it to the best of their ability, primarily using robots. The results were limited. The surface was as resistant as ever to mechanical impact as well as transillumination, and the astronauts had to settle for analyzing it from the outside. The most significant result remained the zoi's reaction to the presence of a human.

After the first encounter, physical contact was no longer necessary. Whenever someone came within a few meters of the zoi, an airlock would open. A human sized cavity emerged in the otherwise impenetrable surface, staying open as long as the person remained nearby, and then closing.

The touch or closeness of a robot prompted no reaction. If a robot was directed into a cavity which had opened for a human, it was gently pushed out. With nothing to latch on to, it would eventually slide off, as everything did on the zoi. Everything except humans. Their closeness made the zoi open up and invite them in. But no astronaut accepted the invitation.

"Why don't they just get in?" I asked Karim, for something like the tenth time.

"They have to be cautious," he patiently explained. "No one knows what will happen if they enter that airlock. It's much too dangerous."

"But the zoi won't hurt them! It just wants to get to know them. Can't they see that?"

"We don't know that, Amira."

Karim tousled my hair, as if I were a little kid. I angrily pushed him away.

"Yes, we can! *I* know. If it were me, I wouldn't be scared. I would do it."

"Then it's too bad you aren't there," he replied with a smile I wasn't sure how to interpret. It wasn't always easy to tell if Karim was being ironic, or if he meant what he said. "Twelve is a little young for an astronaut. But maybe you'll get the opportunity some other time."

"And what if there won't *be* another opportunity?

What if this is the last zoi we ever see? Maybe it leaves tomorrow and another one never comes!"

"Yes, maybe. Maybe it stays here indefinitely, or others keep coming, and in twenty years you get to visit one of them."

"Twenty years?" I stared at him, mouth open.

"Well, fifteen, perhaps, if you really dig your heels in. You don't become an astronaut overnight. It takes hard work and a very long time."

Giving no reply, I slouched down into a chair and stared into space while contemplating my future. I could easily picture myself as an astronaut, but the long road presumably leading there seemed completely abstract. However, I was old enough to understand that Karim was right. Meeting a zoi could remain a childish daydream, but it could also become a reality, if I was ready to make the necessary effort. I resolved to take that path, no matter how long it turned out to be.

AQUARIUM

Kiah created her own residence in the habitat's system of passageways and cavities. In addition to her bedchamber, she has several rooms in which she works on zoi materials as well as her original task: studying the zoi from a psychological and communicative perspective. The zois aren't sentient in any human sense of the word, but they react to stimuli with something resembling purposeful behavior. A behavior we can interact with.

I search through all her rooms without finding her. Knowing that it's probably to no avail, I attempt to call her transmitter, and no, she doesn't answer. Why won't she wear the thing? It's irresponsible. Someone might urgently need to contact her. Like I do right now.

I continue, first towards the toilet and then to the pantry. She's not there either. It's possible she has been in one of those places and then gone back to her own quarters. Evardo looks up as I once again pass through the living room. I look at him questioningly, and he shakes his head. He still hasn't seen her.

Where can she be? I search every part of the habitat. The shadow is with me all the way, attached to my right side, and I do my best to use only my left hand and foot when pushing myself forward, while keeping a distance to the surroundings on the other side. No matter how unsettled I am by the shadow, I'm still afraid of accidentally harming it. The jelly-like substance seems so fragile. I haven't yet had the time or courage to investigate how it's connected to me, but it does more than just stick to my clothes, my instinct tells me that much. If it gets hurt, it will hurt me as well.

Passing through the living room for the third time, I have a whispered conversation with Evardo. He too is mystified, and I can see he's getting concerned. So am I. I envision Kiah's lifeless body, drowned in cytosol fluid or fatally burned by one of the powerful acids from the zoi's digestive system. She was never the cautious type, and since we left the sun, she has become increasingly reckless, convinced that nothing in the zoi will harm her.

Once again, I approach her domain. Maybe she created a new room, and I have overlooked the entrance? I search more thoroughly this time, not just for her, but for something that looks like an opening.

I find nothing in the passageway or the bigger rooms, but in the bedchamber I notice a spot on the wall. It's a circular area about half a meter in diameter, darker than its surroundings with an uneven structure. That's how the membrane usually looks where it's possible to pass through it, out into the cytosol. Why would Kiah have such an exit point in her bedchamber? Venturing out into the fluid requires a suit with an oxygen supply, and having an opening here, in the room where she floats about each night in her sleep, could be downright dangerous.

I reach in a little further. My hand meets a liquid, substantially thinner than the cytosol, but still a liquid. If Kiah's in there, will I find her drowned, as in my fearful imagination? I pull my hand back. Some of the fluid sticks to it, and little bubbles float into the air. The skin of my hand appears unscathed, and it feels fine too. The fluid doesn't seem to be harmful, at least not in the short term.

First a deep inhalation, then I push off from the opposite wall, towards the dark spot. I feel some resistance from the membrane, but it lets me pass.

The fluid around me is indeed thin, lighter flowing than pure water. It feels pleasant against my skin. I open my eyes, and there's no stinging sensation at all. The pH and salt balance must be close to that of the human body.

Kiah is right in front of me. The sight of her open mouth and eyes sends a jolt of fear through me. An open mouth under water is usually not a good sign. But then she smiles and looks at me, mouthing words that come out somewhat muddled and distorted in the fluid, but I'm able to understand them.

"Breathe, Amira. You can do that."

I shake my head and keep my mouth closed. My lungs are starting to complain about the lack of oxygen, but I'm not having any of that kind of breathing, even if Kiah seems completely fine. No bubbles of air leave her mouth when she speaks, so she must have been here for a while, inhaling and exhaling the fluid with no discernible issue. Her choice, not mine. I gesture towards the membrane behind me. I want us both out of here, right now.

"That really isn't necessary," she says, "We can easily talk in here."

Apparently, she doesn't get how much this freaks me out. And objectively speaking, it shouldn't be worse than so much else I have done. I've even breathed liquid before, during the scuba training that was part of my preparations for the astronaut school entrance exam. But I have absolutely no desire to repeat the experience. More than once, I panicked, convinced that I was suffocating. The instructor managed to calm me down, and I completed the dive—but I felt no triumph in having conquered myself. The anxiety remained in my body for days, along with residues of liquid in my lungs. I almost gave up the idea of becoming an astronaut, and in the years to come, whenever I was plagued with doubt, the memory of that dive would be the first thing that came to mind.

Again, I shake my head. My body demands oxygen, and I want it to be air. I use the resistance of the fluid to turn around and swim towards the exit. Out of the corner of my eye, I see the shadow follow my movement. It looks very faint in here. At the same time, it's making little movements which aren't copies of my own. Probably created by currents in the fluid, but they still make the shadow seem more alive, more autonomous.

When I break through the membrane, I hardly feel any change. The lack of gravity makes the difference between liquid and air less noticeable. My body lacks the certainty that it's safe to inhale, like it would have back on Earth. But I can't hold my breath much longer.

In a gasp, I fill my lungs. Liquid bubbles float around me, and I brush them away from my face with fierce movements. If any of them have entered my respiratory system, I fortunately don't feel it. When I turn towards the membrane, it has already closed again. Several seconds pass before Kiah finally emerges, her face first appearing in the membrane as a mask. Then the rest of her follows in a haze of bubbles. She moves slowly, like a sea creature lazily gliding through the water.

Only now I see her shadow, gelatinous and half

transparent like my own. Liquid flows from it and her, and streams of bubbles emanate from her mouth and nose as she puffs, skillfully like a diver emptying their regulator. She is used to this, that much is evident. Bubbles continue to leak from her nostrils and corners of her mouth while she breathes the air, but it doesn't seem to bother her. The same goes for the presence of the shadow. She looks from mine to her own.

"So, it's not just me," she notes. "Do you all have them?"

I nod silently. I feel sick again. It's too much all at once: discovering the shadows. Worrying, first for Linn and then for Kiah. Finding her in the fluid. Am I heading for a breakdown?

"Interesting." Kiah examines her own shadow with her fingers. Then she turns towards mine. Instinctively, I pull away.

"I'd rather you didn't touch it."

"Why not?" She sounds impatient.

"I don't know. But it feels wrong." My voice trails off. The nausea is getting worse.

"Amira." Her voice is gentle. Suddenly, the old Kiah is present, my friend through more than a decade. I look up and meet her gaze.

"I'm sorry," she says. "This can't be easy for you."

Which part of it? I want to ask. Everything seems absurd, even the familiar sight of Kiah's long, wet hair slowly freeing itself from her head and standing straight up, as wet hair does with no gravity to keep it down. My own hair is tied up in a bun, but a few strands have come loose and stand on end in a similar way. I always keep my hair tied back, mostly because it's practical, but also because it feels a bit more normal. During my first visits to space I let my hair flow freely around my head, emphasizing the experience of weightlessness which was still a victory in and of itself. The same weightlessness is now a given that I feel no need to celebrate. Kiah's hair is always loose. When dry, it forms a large, unruly afro which never seems to get in her way.

"A lot of things aren't easy," I say more firmly. I'm tempted to seize the rare moment of intimacy, let my inner chaos out and seek comfort from Kiah. But I don't trust her sympathy to last. "I'm not the one who has it the worst. Linn is badly afflicted. She and Evardo are waiting for us in the living room."

"Waiting? Why?"

"Because this is something we need to investigate together! Hasn't that thought occurred to you?"

It takes a while before she responds, which probably means that she hasn't spared a thought for the rest of us, focusing solely on her own experience.

"I hadn't gotten that far yet," she finally answers. "I had only just begun to examine it. How it reacts to various environments."

Is that meant to be an explanation? We are supposedly a crew, a team. When strange things happen, her first instinct should be seeking out the rest of us. But she no longer thinks that way. She has become a stranger to us. To me.

"I've been looking for you all over the place. You should have told us about..." As so often in the zoi I'm at a loss for a suitable word. "...the aquarium in there."

Kiah lets out a laugh. "The aquarium! Let's just call it that. And of course, I meant to tell you about it. I just wanted to understand it a little better before I did."

You didn't want us to interfere. I don't say it out loud. Instead, I ask:

"How did it emerge? It can't have been there for long. At least not the connection to it."

Kiah frowns. Another thing she seems not to have thought about. She just accepted that the liquid was there, and she has been studying it without a hint of fear or doubt.

"It must have formed in a way similar to the air bubbles," she says. "They were created by the zoi to fill our needs, and this is a new version. Another way to take in oxygen that better suits the environment."

My insides chill. "Do you think that the zoi will replace all the air with liquid?"

The mere thought provokes the feeling of suffocation. Breathing liquid for a limited duration is one thing. If necessary, I suppose I could do that again. But doing it all the time...

"At some point it possibly will." Kiah sounds totally unaffected. "It aligns with our theories. At first, the zoi will focus on creating an environment in which the foreign life form can survive. We need oxygen, and initially it's simpler to provide us with it in the form we are accustomed to. But over time, it's reasonable for the zoi to change it into a form better suited to its own organism."

"Reasonable!?" It comes out as a shrill cry. "I don't care what's reasonable! If the air disappears—if we only have liquid to breathe... I can't do that. I can't live like that."

Kiah watches me coolly, all sympathy vanished, precisely as I expected.

"You may have to. Air-filled spaces aren't natural for the zoi. It must take a lot of energy to sustain them, and they could be harmful to it in the long run. We are its guests, and we are here on its terms. You have known that all along."

Yes, I have. I have entered this with my eyes open, knowing full well that I would spend the rest of my life in an alien environment neither I nor my crewmates are able to control. It was a decision I made after two expeditions to other zois, the most recent one lasting close to a year. I knew what it meant to live in a zoi, and I knew to expect continuous changes, in the environment as well as myself.

I say nothing, as there's nothing to say. After a while, Kiah turns towards the entrance of the bedchamber.

"We should probably join the others."

The shadow lingers beside me like a threat as I follow her. It, too, probably represents some kind of profound change. I still have no idea what it entails. That in itself is frightening.

VISIT

Shortly after the astronauts left it, the second zoi broke its orbit around the sun and set course for interstellar space. It had stayed for roughly the same duration as the first zoi, just under two years.

Four years passed before a third zoi was detected, shortly after my sixteenth birthday. For days I thought of nothing else. Mentally, I was living among the teams of scientists, engineers, and astronauts now working feverishly to prepare another expedition. In the long run, of course, I couldn't turn my back on my own life. If I truly wanted to be an astronaut, I had to keep up with my schoolwork. I had to settle for following the preparations in my meager spare time.

Eleven months after the first observations of zoi number three, the expedition was on its way. This crew was prepared for the invitation which last time had come as a surprise. If this zoi also invited them in, they would heed the call.

However, they weren't planning to embark directly upon a visit. The space shuttle carried a selection of smallish life forms, such as insects, plants, fungal growths, and algae. The results from last encounter showed the zoi responding to the presence of a human, but perhaps the same would apply to other living creatures?

That theory turned out to be correct. Like its predecessors, this zoi rejected purely mechanical robots and probes, but if they contained some kind of life, the zoi reacted exactly as it did to a human. A cavity opened, and once the small craft had entered it, the surface closed around it. The contact to the first probes was immediately lost, but after some experimentation with different types of signals, one of them proved able to penetrate the zoi's shell.

The probes now remained controllable, and they were able to transmit recordings and measurement data. Through the transmissions, the astronauts—and later, everyone else—could observe how the airlock's cavity filled with liquid and then open to the other side, in towards the zoi. Here the probes entered a large, fluid-filled space, intersected by various structures and elements, all seemingly organic in nature. Between them, what looked like independent creatures of various shapes and sizes were swimming around. Some of them would roam the entire zoi, others would shuttle between specific structures or stay within a limited area.

The zoi was inhabited, or so it seemed. But none of the inhabitants displayed any interest in the foreign elements emitted by the airlock. If a probe got in their way, they simply maneuvered around it. Apart from that, they didn't react to its presence.

Now, the question was whether the probes were able to get back out.

After some experimentation, it turned out that persistent, repetitive pressure on the inside of the surface would make a cavity appear. Reversely mirroring the entrance process, the cavity would first close itself off towards the inside of the zoi, and then contract around the probe, emptying itself of the fluid. Then the lock would open again, towards space. The zoi's surface let the life-carrying probes pass in and out. You had to assume that the same would go for people.

Once again, I observed from afar, via the cameras filming from the astronauts' helmets and the microphones recording what they said. I suspect it was broadcasted with some delay. If something disastrous happened, we wouldn't have been allowed to witness it. But all went well.

One astronaut went through an airlock, then a second one followed. They met inside, swimming in the fluid, with movements somewhat hampered by the spacesuits made for empty space, but safe enough.

Like the probes, they quickly encountered what

could easily be taken for inhabitants: biological entities moving around purposefully, still supremely indifferent to the new arrivals. Swimming around any obstacle blocking their way, human or otherwise, remained their only reaction, even when the astronauts made direct attempts at contact.

I followed these attempts, heart pounding. *Please answer*, I thought. *Notice us!* Countless stories had foreseen this moment; the first close encounter with an extraterrestrial being. How many, if any, had imagined that we would simply be ignored? That the space aliens didn't seem to care about our existence?

The two astronauts remained in the zoi for about an hour and then departed, bringing samples of the fluid and other substances that they had collected with the utmost caution. Over the next few weeks, they would take turns making several visits to the zoi, none lasting longer than a few hours. Simultaneously, they started analyzing the samples, soon ascertaining that the zoi shared the most fundamental aspects of its biological makeup with life on Earth.

The basic building blocks were the same: amino acids arranged into proteins. But the cell structure differed from ours, among other things by being fairly diverse, and by not having exactly the same kind of genetic material. All zoi cells did have systems of molecules corresponding quite closely to RNA and DNA, but the information they contained was transferred and applied in ways the biologist in the crew couldn't immediately recognize. They also seemed to vary a great deal.

Back on Earth, I absorbed every drop of information reaching the public. Each held a piece of the answer to the question of life's origin: how, when and where had it emerged? Did it exist elsewhere in the universe, and in what forms? Would alien life resemble us enough that we could interact, or would it be fundamentally different?

The arrival of the first zoi had established that life existed out there, not just on other planets, but in space itself. Now we could also observe that, in its most basic structure, it resembled us. Did that mean we had a common origin, or was the similarity due to some inherent laws applying to life as a phenomenon?

The science of xenobiology had now truly emerged, with an empiric foundation to work from. It was the science I would choose, both for its own sake and for its potential to advance an astronaut career.

COPIES

"To me, it's pretty obvious what they are."

The statement comes from Kiah. We have joined Evardo in the living room, exchanging observations of the shadows. Linn is still asleep, at some distance from the rest of us. The sight of an unconscious person hovering in the air has an eerie feel to it, even when you're used to zero g. But I catch myself envying Linn. I would be such a relief, just going to sleep and forgetting all about the shadows. I might even hope they'd be gone when I woke up.

"Obvious, you say?" Evardo raises his eyebrows.

"Yes—they are copies of us. Clones under construction. They have the rudimentary shape of a body, with the onset of a central nervous system, circulation, and internal organs. In some spots, bones are beginning to form; rapidly growing and developing. When I discovered my shadow this morning, it was barely visible. Now it's hard to overlook."

I'm not sure who first started calling them shadows. Maybe the same word occurred to all of us independently. Kiah is not alone in her theory. I had the same thought, but I didn't want to think it through. Kiah has no problem with that, and Evardo approaches the matter with his usual calm.

"You are probably right that they are human bodies," he says. "But does that necessarily make them copies?"

"Not necessarily, no. But it seems like the logical thing to assume."

Kiah turns comfortably in the air, followed by her shadow. Her hair is still damp, but her naked skin has long since dried. My own clothes cling to me, just like the shadow. I feel a sudden urge to get them off, to let my skin breathe. Why am I wearing clothes at all? The temperature and humidity of the habitat makes it more of a hassle than a benefit. Modesty isn't a factor either, as it has by now become evident that the zoi is hormonally suppressing all sexual urges. But I'm not even sure I will be able to take off my clothes, or if they have become fused between me and the shadow.

"What makes it logical?" Evardo asks.

"That it will be much simpler than building a new individual. The zoi is still familiarizing itself with the workings of the human organism."

I cut in: "It sounds like you know what it's

thinking."

"I don't," Kiah calmly replies. "Mainly because it doesn't think."

"Are we so sure about that?" My voice sounds sharp. "Perhaps it *is* sentient, in a way we can't decipher. It has lured us in. Now we're completely in its power, and it can do whatever it has been planning all along."

I'm heading towards an argument, which is a very bad idea under the circumstances, but I'm not able to stop it. At least, I don't want to.

"Do you really believe that the zoi has malicious intentions?" Kiah doesn't raise her voice, but there's a hint of sarcasm in it. "In all our years of studying the zois together, you and I have argued against this exact mindset: that because this being is alien and incomprehensible to us, we should by default consider it hostile."

You and I. I don't know if she's intentionally referring to our friendship, but in any case, it angers me. Because that friendship no longer exists. She chose to leave it behind.

"Perhaps we were wrong. Perhaps we've been naive and let ourselves be caught in a trap. The zoi has devoured us, transformed us—and now it's cloning us. Once it has those clones, it will no longer need us. Then, what do you think will happen to us?"

"Amira." It comes from Evardo. "We don't understand what's happening, but working yourself up won't help."

The admonishing tone sounds exactly like my father's. The fact that Evardo is probably right doesn't make it any better.

"Then what am I supposed to do? Just pretend like everything's fine? We're at the mercy of a being we don't understand. Sure, it provides us with air and nourishment, but the very same air and nourishment are altering our internal chemistry in a way that's completely outside our control. Linn's body can't tolerate those changes, and you, Kiah—" I pause for a moment, then continue: "Perhaps you tolerate them a little too well. I think you may be transforming into something not quite human."

I want her to get angry, but she just watches me with a faint smile.

"It's true that I'm very much at ease here. And I trust the zoi. Not its conscious intentions, as it doesn't have any, but the mechanisms causing it to create the best possible conditions for other life forms."

I remember the blind, childish faith I used to have in the zois. How purposefully I brought myself into this situation.

"Well, I don't trust it," I say. "Not anymore. And I don't trust that thing."

My face twists with disgust when I look at the elongated, wobbly lump of biological material beside me. Its bodily character has grown more apparent, which only makes it more uncanny. I'm not sure which thought is worse, that it will develop into a monstrous imitation of a human being, or that it will become a true copy of me.

"These shadows are a deeply fascinating phenomenon," Kiah says. "I intend to follow their formation closely—but if they frighten you so much, I should probably focus on my own. At least until you all have settled down a bit."

She reaches for the wall, pushes off, and floats away, in the direction of her own territory. I'm sure she's happy to be rid of our company. Whatever she is evolving into, it doesn't seem to need human contact. The zoi is enough for her. Perhaps the two are more closely connected than she will admit.

Evardo looks like he's unsure which of us to turn his aesculapian common sense towards. The choice seems to fall on me, as he lets Kiah pass and looks at me.

"Amira, I understand if you're struggling to cope with this. It frightens me too, but we must respond to it rationally, for the sake of everybody involved."

Now he looks past me, towards Linn who is beginning to stir. Of course, he will use her as an argument. She's worse off than me, therefore I need to pull myself together. I tighten my lips, turn around and push off in her direction.

"Linn," I say softly. "How are you doing?"

She moans, probably from nausea; opens her eyes and gazes first at me, then my shadow.

"They are still here." She takes a trembling breath. "And they have grown bigger."

I refrain from commenting. "Come," I say instead. "Let's go look at the stars. It helps with most things."

Gently, I wrap my arm around her. I'm just able to do so without touching her shadow, which is attached to her left side, while mine is to the right. She looks around bewildered, and her gaze finds Evardo. For a moment I think he will interfere, but either he's afraid of my reaction, or he recognizes that we need to get our minds off the current situation.

It's a bit awkward towing us both through the air, but I manage to move Linn to the passageway leading to the holoroom, and in there it's easier to push us forward. Besides, Linn has regained some composure, and she helps with the movement. Perhaps it calms her to feel my body against hers. That's how I feel myself. I don't let go of her until we have arrived.

In the holoroom, I start getting the equipment ready. A simple video message, like the one from Nathan, we will usually watch in daylight, but when it comes to regular holo footage, especially projections from the outside, the room needs to be darkened. For this purpose, I activate the balloon, a black membrane that slowly unfolds and closes itself around us.

Complete darkness is unknown inside the zoi. Like the ones we previously visited, this zoi quickly established a cycle of night and day that closely aligns with the earthly twenty-four hours. But even in the nighttime, some measure of bioluminescence is always present. True darkness has become a luxury which I now relish.

The projector's control panel lightens up. I start adjusting it, but then I feel Linn's hand on mine.

"Let me do it," she says.

I pull back, letting her connect the projector to the telescope on the outside. In our initial attempts to implant electronics into the surface of the zoi, it first kept repelling the foreign objects, like it had done with the probes our predecessors tried to send in. Eventually, we succeeded in getting one to stick. The fact that the equipment was composed of biologically based materials might have been of significance. But the crucial thing was probably the persistent repetition, signaling that this was imperative to its guests.

The telescope connects us with the stars. This isn't just important because of the data we gather this way, but also because of the sensory link to the surroundings. It lets us follow the zoi's movement through space, even though we cannot influence it. Without the telescope, we would be prisoners in a small, confined space. With it, we're astronauts heading for other solar systems.

Linn and I seek each other out in the darkness, and we hold each other while the stars ignite around us—the stars we're traveling towards, and the star we are leaving behind. All of them are incredibly far away, and yet we are amidst them. Inside the zoi, we live among the stars. It's the fulfillment of a dream, for each of us, as well as for all of humanity. For so long, it has been unreachable. Now it has come true.

Isn't that worth the price, whatever it may be?

TOUCH

The years between the third and fourth zoi were an intense time for me. I was seventeen when zoi number three departed, and twenty-three when number four approached the solar system. It is a period of your life where you focus on seeking new experiences, educating yourself, and shaping your identity. I did all these things, trying to cram as much as possible into the available time. I strived to get through my biology studies quickly, but still with the best possible results, simultaneously taking courses in flying, diving, first aid, and crisis management—anything that might improve my chances of getting into astronaut school.

Becoming an astronaut is statistically nigh impossible. Thousands of applicants per vacancy have been common ever since the early decades of space exploration. No matter how much I prepared for it, my chances were still minimal. But I would do my utmost, which required a hard effort on multiple fronts.

My parents were ambivalent about my dreams for the future. They appreciated my determination, but they would have preferred it to lead in a somewhat different direction. Biology research was a perfectly decent career path. If it absolutely had be xenobiology, my career could still take place on Earth. There were ample employment opportunities in the analysis of data others brought back from space. Why not just keep to that?

Their generation had grown up in an unsettled world, marked by climate disasters, wars, and political unrest. These unpredictable conditions made stability a paramount priority. My family had navigated those tumultuous years by sticking together and consistently choosing the safest path. They couldn't comprehend why you would want anything else out of life. They had expected me to outgrow my childish fantasies of space travel and alien encounters, and they were deeply concerned that, like Karim, I was rejecting the security they had worked so hard to attain.

Karim helped me out as best he could, not just by supporting me within the family, but also by securing assistant positions for me on various research and emergency aid projects, providing me with valuable experience.

At the age of twenty-two, I had obtained an undergraduate degree as a biologist, and I applied to astronaut school for the first time. I didn't get in, which was exactly as expected. Hardly anyone was admitted on their first attempt, and I would just have to try again. Still, there was no guarantee that I would ever succeed.

Five years had passed since the last zoi's departure. This was longer than in the earlier instances, and I wasn't the only one getting worried. Astronomers were uncertain how to interpret the pattern. Perhaps the zois had always visited our solar system at regular intervals, and we just hadn't noticed them. They were small enough to have been overlooked. The long wavelength radio waves they emitted could easily have been absorbed by Earth's atmosphere, and space telescopes large enough to image these wavelengths had only come into use a few years prior to the discovery of the first zoi. But it was equally possible that the zois formed a cluster; some astronomers used the word *swarm*, as if they were insects connected across cosmic distances. And such a swarm or cluster would sooner or later have passed us. It might already have happened.

The astronauts, who had visited the previous zoi, left behind various devices to continue collecting data and transmitting it back home. After a week's time, those instruments had begun reporting damage, and shortly after, the signals stopped coming. Either the zoi environment was more detrimental to the tech than first estimated, or the zoi had deliberately destroyed it. Perhaps because it regarded the instruments as foreign objects, or simply because it had consumed the minerals and compounds they consisted of. In any case, another attempt to examine the alien being through purely technological means had failed. All we could do was wait and hope for the arrival of another zoi.

Finally, the first observations of a new specimen were made, questionable at first, but gradually more conclusive. I felt relieved, delighted, and at the same time frustrated to once again be watching from the sidelines. This time, though, I had company. Everyone at the graduate research program I was now enrolled in was intent on grasping every detail. We gathered for joint presentations in holographic auditoriums, equipped with state-of-the-art gear. It was almost, but only almost, like being there yourself.

The first course of events was a repetition of the previous expedition: Probes carrying simple life forms were sent in, and when there was no sign of danger, the astronauts followed suit. Measurements from the inside of both this and the previous zoi revealed a radiation level considerably lower than in the space shuttle. The organic surface seemed to provide much better protection against cosmic rays than any man-made shielding. Nothing prevented the astronauts from staying inside the zoi for longer intervals, such as a whole day. During this time, they studied the surroundings, collected samples and made renewed attempts at communicating with the freely swimming entities that were present in this zoi as well.

Those attempts yielded no results, but another, entirely unplanned, act did.

The astronaut later claimed that she had acted on a whim while analyzing the surrounding fluid. The fact that she was a chemist may have been of some significance. Someone in another occupation might not have felt as confident that the fluid was harmless to her. But curiosity can be a powerful drive, and people who have chosen space exploration as a career are particularly prone to it.

She took off her glove.

The incident wasn't broadcasted in real time, and by the time I watched the recording, I already knew what had happened. Still, I got goosebumps all over my body. A direct touch, skin against liquid. The astronaut and the camera following her gaze observed her hand wriggling free from the glove. The spacesuit was designed to make each part easily changeable, and the sleeve sealed tightly around her wrist. Only her hand came into contact with the fluid.

The shouting from the other astronauts has been edited out of the publicly accessible recordings, but I heard it later. It didn't take long, though, before their consternation was replaced by intrigue, as the touch didn't seem to have any adverse effect. The chemist's health condition was carefully monitored through the suit, and this monitoring displayed no reaction, neither in her skin nor anywhere else in her system. But shortly afterwards, something looking like a reaction from the zoi could be registered:

It had started making air.

It seemed to emerge from the liquid itself. Small bubbles appeared near the chemist, and when a few other astronauts followed suit and removed a glove, the same thing happened: The liquid around them was punctured by bubbles which grew and merged into larger pockets of air. These pockets gradually developed a surface which retained the air but remained permeable. Analysis of the air revealed it to be pure oxygen. Not ideal for long term breathing, but harmless in the short run.

Some of the air-filled spaces soon became large enough to contain a human body. Another invitation. This time, it was immediately accepted.

Again, the chemist took the lead, now acting in agreement with the rest of the crew. She entered an air pocket, opened her helmet, and took a few breaths. Then she gave a thumbs up. All good.

Not long afterwards, measurements indicated changes in all air accumulations. The oxygen was accompanied by other gasses, gradually approaching the composition of the Earth's atmosphere. More astronauts experimented with breathing inside the air pockets which were now converging into a system interconnected by passages. The whole structure grew. The surrounding membranes became denser and more robust, except from a few areas still allowing passage. The zoi had created a home for its guests.

Back at the University, we debated this in a rush of excitement. Evidently, something inside the zoi was reading the biology of its guests, analyzing their needs and attempting to accommodate them. Did this happen automatically, or did it imply some kind of conscious intent? In any case, a more favorable contact between two species so alien to each other was hardly fathomable. An amiable conversation. Do you need this? Here you are. You are welcome here.

I was no longer a child, filled with wide-eyed notions about encounters with beings from space. Yet, that very thing was now a reality. Perhaps not exactly as I had imagined, but still, the friendly, glowing creature really *was* friendly. It invited us in. We were as strange to it as it was to us, but still it tried to get to know us, more fundamentally than any verbal communication could ever achieve.

Did it feel that we responded to it?

BUBBLES

The shadows are growing. My shadow, Linn's shadow and presumably Kiah's and Evardo's too, but I rarely see them. Linn and I are together almost constantly. Being alone with the shadow is eerie. An unfinished, adult-sized body, still partially translucent, containing a growing number of recognizable structures such as blood vessels, bones, muscles, and internal organs, but without skin. It's directly connected to me at the hip and the shoulder, while the rest of the shadow body has loosened itself from me as it took shape. The sight evokes a mixture of disgust and an equally sickening empathy for this skinless condition. The shadow seems so vulnerable, and at the same time frighteningly vital.

When Linn is around, I can handle its presence. Sometimes I almost forget about it because I have her to hold onto. Together we sleep, talk, watch the stars or holofilms from Earth. Our DNA-based data storage contains an abundance of them, together with something resembling all the information and entertainment available at the time of our departure. Usually, we choose sequences without any action; footage of landscapes, of cities filled with people; the environments we left behind for the sake of the zoi and the stars.

We hold and caress each other, naked because wearing clothes has become a practical impossibility, and the fabrics feel unpleasant against our oddly hypersensitive skin. This hypersensitivity does not apply to the skin of another person. Quite the reverse, we have a strong need for physical intimacy. It isn't sex, as our bodies have stopped responding sexually, but the sensual pleasure of touch remains intact.

"Let me know if you want some time on your own."

I hover in front of the entrance to her bedchamber while she is entering. We have just completed a holographic tour of the Alps in the adjacent room, and it's not that I feel any desire to be alone, but Linn usually keeps to herself quite a lot.

Inside, she turns around and shakes her head vigorously.

"Not at all. I want you here. It helps."

"On your health, too?" I ask. "You usually claim to need peace and quiet."

Linn reaches out through the opening and pulls

me in. It shouldn't take much of an effort, but she looks as if it's a strain.

"That's because it was so hard to keep up the facade," she says. "I didn't want you to see how weak I was."

I close the opening behind me.

"We knew. At least, we've known for a while."

"Of course. But we could all pretend it wasn't that bad."

Linn's bedchamber is larger than mine, and she has done a much better job arranging it, principally by molding multiple cavities into the wall membrane, customized in size and shape to the items she stores in them. Just like the entrance to the room, they can be sealed completely. Her belongings never float around in the air, unless she forgets to put them away.

"Why did you need to pretend?" I ask.

"Pride." She sighs. "I could never admit defeat. I must be capable of everything, or I am nothing."

I recognize that feeling. That's exactly why I initially felt somewhat uneasy around Linn. She had accomplished everything I had told myself was impossible: being accepted at astronaut school on the first try, at the age of twenty-three, already holding a Ph.D. in BB-tech, after racing through the education system at record speed. She could have reached the very top in academia or the corporate world, or both, but she turned her back on it all, to venture into space and study the zois.

Would I have been as stubborn as Linn if I had the same difficulties with adapting to the surroundings? Would I have covered up my symptoms so I wouldn't be passed over? When it was too late to undo my choice, would I have strived as hard to conceal how weak I truly was? I'm not sure if I would or not. And I'm not sure what to think about it either. In a way, I admire Linn for her ironclad determination, but it didn't lead to anything good, for her or for the rest of us.

I move towards her.

"If you had let go of that facade, it would have been easier for us to help you."

"I know." She closes her eyes, letting her body float as best it wants. Next to her, the shadow mirrors her movements—to a certain extent, as the eyes are only partially formed, and the shadow doesn't have any eyelids yet. I try to avoid looking at it, though this is getting harder as the shadows approach the size of a regular body.

A faint smile forms on Linn's face. "It *is* a relief to let go of the facade," she says. "To let everything go. I no longer need to hide anything, at least not from you."

It's true. We have opened to each other in a way that seems almost childlike. An intense intimacy that I recognize from friendships and crushes of my childhood and teens; perhaps also from the early part of my relationship with Natan, although this had a different character. Natan and I took our time getting to know each other. Right now, it seems like Linn and I are trying to get under each other's skin as quickly as possible.

I assume that Linn is drifting off to sleep. She sleeps multiple times throughout the day, sometimes just for a few minutes, sometimes for hours. But she opens her eyes again and looks at me.

"What do you think will happen?" she asks. "When they are... finished, I mean."

Usually, the shadows are the only thing we never talk about, unless some practicality forces us to recognize their presence.

"I don't know."

"And you don't want to know," she states. "Neither do I. Even asking the question is difficult. Why do we feel that way? We should be busy examining them."

"I'm sure Kiah and Evardo are."

"Then we ought to assist them. Instead, we're hiding."

I suppose we are. Two astronauts, trained to keep our heads cool in the most extreme conditions. Whatever is happening to us, we should be facing it, not trying to repress it. But it's all I'm able to do.

"I assume we can blame our hormones," Linn continues when I don't respond. "The zoi is messing with them in a way that influences our behavior."

"But hasn't it been like that for you since we

left?"

She shakes her head.

"Not quite. I always feel sick and exhausted, but this is different. I have this powerful urge to do specific things, and to avoid others. For example, I really don't want to discuss the fact that I have those urges."

Neither do I. I'd much rather cuddle up to Linn and talk about something nice and cozy, or just anything else than the situation we're currently in. Linn and I told each other the stories of our lives, from our earliest memories onwards. Of course, we will sometimes talk about life in the zoi, as Linn's struggles with adapting to it is a subject we can hardly avoid. But mostly we keep to the distant past.

"Then why don't Kiah and Evardo react in the same way?" I force myself to ask.

"Because we always react differently. Kiah thrives on anything the zoi exposes her to, and Evardo is such a steady nature. He is not easily affected."

I ought to be just as impervious. Linn is weakened enough to be excused, by I have no justification for burying my head in the sand. Except maybe to claim that I do it for Linn's sake, and that's only partially true.

Linn touches her forehead and then runs her hand down her body. "I'm sweating," she says.

I notice the glistening layer of liquid covering her skin. In some places, there's enough of it for bubbles to form and free themselves.

"Do you have a fever?"

"A mild one, maybe. But primarily, I need to wash."

She turns towards the storage cavity where she keeps the cloths.

"Do you need help?" I ask.

"No, thanks. I'm not that weak."

Not yet. None of us say it out loud, but I'm sure we're both thinking it.

She pulls out a cloth and retrieves a water tube from another cavity. With it, she wets the cloth and starts washing herself, one piece of skin at a time.

I catch myself recalling my experience in Kiah's aquarium. The liquid in it isn't water, and it makes no sense to think of it in terms of a bath. Rather, the aquarium represents a future in which the very concept of bathing is irrelevant. I push the thought aside, and instead I try to remember what a shower felt like. But there's no comfort in that. Showers require gravity, and I'll probably never again feel the water jets hitting my skin and running down my body. Here in the zoi, the only options are sponge baths or a closed room filled with water. Which again reminds me of the aquarium and, consequently, how the air we breathe may at some point be replaced by liquid.

As Kiah says, this would probably work much better for the zoi, and it would make some things easier for us. We would be able to move around without pushing off from anything. In the air, if we can't get a hold of anything to pull or push, we are essentially helpless. Out of reach of any walls or structures, I could in principle be twisting and turning in the air indefinitely, without getting anywhere. In a liquid medium, I would be able to swim, but then I would have to give up one of the few things that works exactly like it does on Earth: breathing.

I hear a snap.

"Damn!" Linn exclaims.

The water tube has cracked. A large bubble detaches from the container and floats in the air. Linn wraps the cloth around it to absorb some up the liquid.

"Don't worry about it," I say, kicking my way to the cavity which holds the tubes. "I'll get you another one."

"Sooner or later, we'll run out of them. I was supposed to have developed an alternative by now."

She's on the verge of tears. Producing replacements out of zoi material for all the equipment we have brought from Earth was Linn's most important task. She hasn't been able to fulfill it.

"Linn, you've been ill. No one blames you for that."

I return with the tube. She takes it without opening it.

"I do," she says. Tears have started to form in her eyes. More water bubbles in the air. Some of them collide with the large one and get absorbed into it. "It's pathetic. I shouldn't be so weak. I should have been able to overcome it. Now I'm just dead weight."

"You aren't dead weight, Linn! I'm glad you're here, especially now, so we're in this together." I nod towards out respective shadows.

"I'm sure you would manage without me. Perhaps you would even be better at facing it. I infect you with my weakness."

"Linn..."

I hold her, letting her cry. There's nothing I can say, except what I already said. By now it seems unlikely that she will ever get better. It's probably not any comfort to her that Kiah is well on her way to taking over her responsibilities.

Things are how they are. Linn is here, together with me, for as long as it lasts. If I blame her for anything, it's not her weakness, but her unwillingness to admit to it. She should never have come, but she probably isn't able to handle that thought. I can hardly handle it myself.

LOVE

I met Natan when I was twenty-five years old, on an expedition to the Cayman Trench in the Caribbean Sea which Karim had helped me get into. The objective was deep-sea exploration, primarily with underwater drones, but a few manned vessels would also be deployed—and with a little luck, I would be on one of them.

It was as close as you got to space travel without leaving the planet. The Cayman Trench isn't among the deepest, but it contains black smokers, hydrothermal vents emitting a dark column of sulfurous minerals and water heated to temperatures above 400 °C. Still, there's life down there.

Natan was a marine biologist who was currently specializing in deep-sea life forms. Like me, he was following a graduate research program, and he was engrossed in his field in a way that fascinated me. Of course, I too was captivated by the subject of my studies, but these studies still had a very specific goal. Natan's sole focus was absorbing knowledge. He wasn't concerned with the concept of having a career but went from project to project driven by pure interest, and he was always eager to expand the scope of this interest.

Deeply focused, he listened to everything I told him about the zois, the factual part as well as my childhood memories. Being slightly younger than me, and not having had someone like Karim, Natan didn't remember the arrival of the first zoi. To him, the zois were just one among many fascinating examples of life's ability to exist under extreme circumstances.

In long and intense conversations, we discussed our fields of study along with various other topics. When I went on a deep dive into the trench, Natan was the one supporting me from the boat. Personally, he never boarded any of the small underwater vessels used to investigate the hydrothermal vents. Being there himself wasn't important to him.

It wasn't until the expedition ended that we realized we had fallen in love. We returned to our respective corners of the world but kept calling and writing each other several times a day. Still, we missed each other terribly. He visited me, and suddenly we were in bed, doing something completely different from talking.

I had been in relationships before, but never felt

this kind of connection with another person. Both our differences and similarities bound us together. We were engaged in nearly the same subjects, though in contrasting ways. I wanted to venture out and encounter other life forms, he was fine with studying them at a distance, through recordings and data brought home by others. Consequently, he was the one to move to my place, as it wasn't that important to him where in the world he was situated.

At that time, I had recently moved to Australia where ETLEA had its headquarters. Though the organization had set up astronaut academies in other places, the one in Australia was the largest, and preparatory courses were easy to find in the area. Shortly before I met Natan, I had applied for a second time, once again without success. The admission procedures were held at two-year intervals, and next time I would put everything into getting accepted. In order to concentrate fully on preparing for the procedures, I wouldn't do any research or teaching, only taking odd jobs to supplement my savings.

It worked. I was accepted into the school, and one year later, I was employed by ETLEA. Officially, I was now an astronaut, even though I hadn't yet left Earth for more than brief intervals.

Natan was immensely proud of me. For long stretches of time, we saw very little of each other, either because I was away or because I came home utterly exhausted. But whenever I had the energy to tell him about my experiences, he would listen with unbridled enthusiasm. If, back then, he was already pondering our future, he probably brushed any worries aside. At least, it wasn't a topic we ever discussed.

When I thought about the future, I only considered the part taking place in space. The next zoi, provided one showed up. The next expedition, which I could only hope to be selected for. We were a lot of people sharing the same burning desire, and even within ETLEA, not everyone could have it fulfilled.

One and a half years passed, then we were informed that another zoi was on its way.

Once again, the odds were that I wouldn't be chosen. Only seven astronauts would take part in the expedition, and at least three would be found among participants of the previous missions. That left four spots, which ten times as many people were competing for, all of them as least as qualified as me. But I was among the four who got selected.

This expedition would be of longer duration. We were to stay inside the zoi, not just for a day at a time, but for several days or even weeks. This was on the assumption that the zoi would welcome us, like its predecessors had. We couldn't know for sure if it would create air pockets for us, but we assumed it would. So far, all the zois had behaved in exactly the same way, and the geneticists studying the samples from the latter two had established that they were identical. Even allowing for the risk of misjudging the alien genetic material, the resemblance seemed strong enough to justify using the term *clones*.

My own research into the zois had primarily focused on the nature of the collected substances, in combination with recordings and observations of the organism. I adhered to the idea that the zoi was a kind of supercell. As massive as it was, it naturally consisted of smaller cells, but the structure they formed had a lot in common with single-celled organisms as we knew them on Earth. The complex earthly cells, eukaryotes, are in themselves highly advanced forms of life, with a multitude of internal structures and elements, each serving different functions. I believed that this was how we should understand the biological entities swimming around inside the zoi. They corresponded to the motile organelles of the eukaryotes, which explained why they acted more like robots than independent beings. They were merely components of a cell.

If the zois behaved like cells, it meant that they reproduced through cell division; a process in which a single specimen turns into two identical copies. Over time, mutations would naturally occur, but since we hadn't yet observed a zoi dividing itself, this seemed to take place relatively rarely. Having only analyzed genetic material from two individuals, we had no way of knowing if only those two happened to be identical.

But I suspected that the similarities were significant. That genetically speaking, it was the same or nearly the same zoi we had encountered each time.

I discussed all of this with Natan, in combination with the practical details of the expedition. Naturally, we would also talk of other things, and we did things together that had nothing to do with biology or space exploration. As absorbed as I was in my work, I knew that you shouldn't neglect your private life. Natan and I attended concerts and performances, went on hikes, socialized with family and friends. My parents and Natan liked each other a lot, and I enjoyed visiting his family, which was larger than mine. It consisted of a number of complex constellations involving current, former and simultaneous relationships between people who all got along with each other surprisingly well.

Natan and I had it all—love, friendship, sex, shared interests. Maybe we didn't spend as much time together as most couples, but when we did, we truly cherished it. I was about to achieve what I had been striving for my entire life, and Natan was pursuing his own dreams. His aspirations were more diverse than mine, involving a multitude of projects, some of them purely scientific, others encompassing aspects of nature restoration, art, humanitarian work, or a blend of it all. He was involved with the local community where we lived. I didn't have time for that kind of thing, but I admired his efforts, just as he admired my focus on a single goal.

We loved and respected each other. At the moment, that seemed to be enough.

SEPARATION

It happens during the night, while I'm asleep—in my own quarters, for the first time in weeks. Both Linn and I feel that we could use a night to ourselves. At least, that's what we tell each other, but really, it's an impulse whose origin I'm unsure of. The kind of urge Linn mentioned, to do something specific. The powerful yearning for closeness has been replaced by an equally powerful need for solitude. Roughly the same feeling I had in the days preceding the materialization of the shadows, only more intense.

The moment I wake up, I realize that something has changed. Something is missing on my right side, the warmth from a body which has in the last few days become increasingly similar to my own, growing skin and hair. A full human being attached to me at the hip and the shoulder. Now, even before I reach for my hip and shoulder to feel around, I know there's nothing there.

I gasp. Behind me, I hear the sound repeated. I turn around.

My own eyes stare back at me.

"No!"

The exclamation doesn't come from me, but from her. The other Amira. The copy.

I dare not move. I don't know which possibility scares me the most—that she will imitate my movements, or that she won't. Right now, she mirrors my immobility. I see my own terror reflected in her face.

Her, not its.

Lately, it has occasionally crossed my mind that perhaps I should think of the shadow as a human being rather than an object. But it has remained silent, continuing to passively mimic every gesture. Until now.

"What... do you want?" Again, it's her.

"What do *I* want?" I exclaim. "I'd like to know what *you* want. And what you are. Did the zoi create you?" I see the confusion in her gaze, and I add: "*Are you the zoi?*"

She shakes her head slowly, with a blank expression on her face. Then she lifts her gaze to look at me again.

"Do you think... that you are me?"

Oh God. She doesn't realize that she is the copy. She believes that *I* am.

"I don't *think* anything," I reply. "I know who I am! I am Amira, and you are something which has been growing alongside me for the last couple of weeks. Some kind of clone. We have been physically connected until now, and you have shown no signs of having your own consciousness. Now you do. But you are still a copy."

That blank expression again. Then she closes her eyes and lets out a laugh.

"That's exactly how it is—except you've got it backwards. *I* am Amira. I have watched the clone grow at my side. I remember it. I remember my entire life. Everything that has led me here."

"So do I."

"But one of us has to be mistaken. One of us must be the copy."

We both fall silent. For a while, we hover there in the bedchamber, in front of each other, like a pair of twins in the womb. Then she grabs onto the wall and pushes herself towards the exit.

"I want out of here!"

That's exactly what I was about to say, but she beat me to it. Well, now I'm rid of her! Maybe I should just stay here, savor the fact that I'm finally truly alone. Only, that will give her every chance to establish herself as the real Amira. And the moment she is out of sight, my body begins to react with a discomfort growing worse by the second. My heart is racing. The blood presses against my eardrums.

There is still a bond between us, and now it is being stretched. It pulls at me.

I resist for maybe a minute, then I follow her.

She is waiting for me in the passageway, breathing rapidly and shallowly, just like I am.

"Okay." It sounds like she's forcing the word out. "We'd better stay together."

We make our way down the passageway towards the living room. I look through the membrane, out towards the busy traffic in the cytosol, with all its diverse entities, each having their own role to play in the zoi organism. Some are in large numbers, others just a few specimens. And now there are two of me.

As I peer into the living room through the entrance, I see them: Evardo and Evardo are hovering beside each other. A distance away, Kiah and Kiah are floating in the air, arms around each other. No sign of Linn. I'll have to check on her later, but right now I want to hear what the others have to say.

Shoulder to shoulder, we push ourselves into the room. The four others glance at us from their respective directions. The Kiahs smile serenely, the Evardos appear somewhat tense, yet significantly more composed than I feel myself. None of them are wearing any clothes. That, too, makes us seem more like elements of the zoi, like pure biology. The clothes were the last remaining layer of culture. Now it has been peeled away.

"I expect you have had the discussion," one of the

Evardos says, "about which of you is the original?"

I nod silently. The other Amira does the same. I guess we both know what Evardo is going to say, but we listen without interrupting.

"It won't lead you anywhere," he continues. "We all have the memory of an entire life, including the last few weeks when we have witnessed the creation of our doppelgänger. It has been passively following us, until this morning when we woke up as two distinct individuals. The two are identical in every aspect, and both are completely convinced they are the true version of themselves."

The other Evardo points to some glass containers floating in the air, with bubbles of liquid inside.

"I have taken some DNA-samples from the two of myself, and they are identical. A replication has taken place, but it is perfect enough that it's impossible to determine which one of us has up to this point been Evardo, and who has been a copy with no independent awareness. Besides, I doubt than an answer to this question would be helpful, precisely because we all are equally certain of our identity."

"Agreed." It comes from one of the Kiahs. The other one adds: "We must accept what has happened and look ahead."

"But we don't understand what happened," I object. "The zoi has replicated us, that much is evident, but we don't know why it did it—or if it may do it again."

The thought makes my stomach churn. Behind the wall membrane of the living room, I see a shoal of energy-transporting organelles pass by. Ranulae, we call them, using the Latin word for tadpole, because that's what they look like: a head-body with a long tail fin attached, moving them forward through the cytosol fluid. I picture a whole flock of me swimming away in a similar fashion, in order to carry out some task or other.

"It's making us a part of its organism," I hear the other Amira say, as if she's expressing my thoughts. "Do we want that? And what will we do if the process repeats itself? There is a limit to how many people we have room for in here."

The two Kiahs exchange glances. One of them turns towards us.

"The zoi is growing bigger. Haven't you noticed?"

Now we are the ones looking at each other, Amira and I. We haven't noticed anything. We have been hiding with Linn, practically cocooning ourselves. Kiah, of course, has undergone the same process with her eyes completely open, not only following the emergence of her own shadow, but also having the surplus energy required to monitor changes in the surroundings.

"No," I say. "How much has it grown?"

"About twenty percent." The two Evardos respond in unison. They both give a start, a conspicuously strong reaction for Evardo. They hesitate for a moment, then one of them continues: "That is the overall increase in volume. It has grown in width as well as length, so it's not just stretching. It is getting larger."

"Furthermore, we are not the only ones being copied," one of the Kiahs add. "Several of the organelles are multiplying in number."

I don't like this at all. My hand reaches out, as it has done so often lately when Linn and I have huddled together. Now my left hand finds its own reflection, the other Amira's right hand. Holding it feels surprisingly good.

"Does it happen the same way?" I ask. "Do they get shadows too?"

"It doesn't look like it. All the organelles swimming around seem fully developed. There are just more of them than usual."

More of them. More of us. There's two of me; that fact overshadows everything else. I know that I—that we—should stay here with the Evardos and the Kiahs and analyze the situation. But I can't, not right now.

"I'll go check on Linn." Other-Amira beats me to the excuse. Her voice sounds strained.

"Yes, do that," an Evardo replies. The other one continues: "Let us know if she needs any help."

I know Evardo well enough to sense the reluctance. They would rather avoid it. The man whose unwavering composure usually annoys me is currently struggling to handle the situation. That has probably been the case all along. The fact that he doesn't seem to know how Linn is doing is odd in itself. He hasn't checked on me since the shadows appeared, and I suspect the same goes for the rest of the crew. After all, he is a doctor, and he should have closely monitored our state of health throughout this strange ordeal. Perhaps he, too, had an impulse to suppress what happened and retreat into his own bubble.

While Other-Amira moves through the entrance to the passageway leading to Linn's quarters, I turn around and look towards the two figures of Kiah. They have let go of each other but maintain eye contact. Personally, I find it difficult to look at my own double.

I contemplate my wrecked friendship with Kiah. We used to understand each other, but I haven't been able to keep up with the change she has been undergoing. All the things I found so hard to handle were effortless and natural to her. She would talk about things I didn't comprehend and probably didn't even want to. Perhaps she also felt lonely when we drifted apart. Now she isn't lonely anymore.

Where does that leave me?

An invisible force pulls at me, compelling me to follow my doppelgänger. No matter how I feel about her existence, it's unbearable to be separated from her. The bond between us isn't build on affection but on a raw, basic need. Keeping my distance from her is like holding my breath. It's possible to do for a while, but sooner or later, instinct will override will. The body takes over.

I resist for another second, then follow her into the passageway.

SOJOURN

My first real sighting of the zoi through the space shuttle's window filled me with childlike joy and wonder. The luminous play of colors looked just as friendly to me as it had when I was five years old sitting on Karim's lap. Ever since that moment, I had dreamed of the encounter that I was now heading towards.

At the same time, it was frightening. In a short while, I would be swallowed up by an alien life form. Twice before, humans had entered a zoi without coming to any harm, but this was no guarantee that things would go just as well the third time. We would be at the mercy of a being we knew next to nothing about. But that was why I was here: to encounter the strange and unknown. A form of life which didn't belong to our planet.

Kiah hovered beside me. She grasped my hand,

and I noticed her own trembling slightly. Like me, she had been captivated by the zois since early childhood. Beyond that, I didn't know much about her, as our friendship had formed during the preparations for the expedition, and the work hadn't left much time for personal conversations. But she was evidently deeply affected.

Everything unfolded as expected. A few probes containing algae were sent in, and the recordings and analyses they conducted revealed that the genetic material was again identical to the samples we had in store. This was another clone. With that established, we were ready to go through the airlocks. Two of the participants from the previous expedition went in first, and Kiah and I followed a couple of days later, while the remaining three crew members stayed aboard the space shuttle, ready to assist us from there.

Even with all the training we had undergone, it was a staggering experience. The surface of the zoi was sucked in, looking more like a gaping maw than an airlock. The dense membrane squeezed tightly around us, making me feel I was choking, even though I had been exposed to much higher degrees of pressure during training sessions. Then the airlock filled with liquid, and the membrane opened before of us, into the zoi.

I had seen it numerous times before, in holograms and VR, but being there myself was an utterly different thing. Still wearing my spacesuit, I swam around in a large, liquid filled space, illuminated by a soft, yet vivid glow that seemed to emanate from everywhere all at once. Strings and grids crisscrossed through the fluid. Here and there, larger structures were visible; some simple, rounded shapes, others composed of intricate coils and twists, with multi-colored layers and parts. Between these structures, a lively coming and going of something looking like a multifarious underwater fauna was unfolding.

For a while, I floated there, so overwhelmed by the alien surroundings that I forgot everything else. Then Kiah's voice called out in my helmet. I looked up to see her spacesuit-clad figure waving at me, next to something I recognized as an air pocket. Through the semi-transparent membrane of the pocket, I caught a glimpse of two human shapes. The other astronauts, Mairi and Sipho.

They helped us penetrate the membrane, entering an air-filled space large enough to contain us all. Both had shed their helmets, and they appeared to be fine. This was the last remaining step: removing my helmet. I paused for a moment, then found the opening mechanism.

The air felt humid and warm. It mostly smelled of human, but behind the familiar odors was one I couldn't identify or compare to anything. The smell of the zoi.

We stayed for four months. At varying intervals, we had a change of guard in which one or two of us changed places with the crew members back at the space shuttle. I spent as much time as I could inside the zoi, despite beginning to feel unwell after a while. We all experienced some degree of physical discomfort, and the doctors back on Earth were far from happy about it. However, the examinations we conducted on ourselves and each other, following the doctors' guidance, didn't indicate any serious health issues. And besides, in the instant we left the zoi, the discomfort would vanish.

Most of the crew preferred staying for shorter durations, but Kiah and I opted for the opposite strategy: sticking it out in the hope it would pass. And it seemed to work. After a week's uninterrupted time in the zoi, Kiah started feeling better. I had to endure twice as long with nausea and fatigue, then it alleviated for me too.

Some kind of adaptation seemed to be happening. Taking breaks from it only dragged it out, and leaving the zoi for longer periods of time made the adaptation roll back. I bitterly regretted a four-day trip to the space shuttle during the third month of our stay, because the nausea hit me again when I returned to the zoi. It passed more quickly this time, but it still wasn't fun.

I didn't have the time for sickness, as there was so much to do. The zoi was a world in itself, one we couldn't possibly manage to explore to a sufficient extent. Using samples, observations, and recordings, we attempted to get as complete a picture of its composition as possible. But it contained so many elements, and the interplay between them was extremely complex.

By now, everybody agreed that the zoi should be viewed as a single organism. Nothing in it seemed to act out of self-interest. Every component, the fixed as well as the freely swimming, had very specific functions, and though we had only worked out a fraction of those, all activity followed predictable patterns, which we were registering and describing.

Among the first functions we identified were those of digestive organs: a system of membrane-enclosed vessels, of which the outermost segment, closest to the cell wall, contained fragments of rocks in various degree of dissolution. The dissolved substance would pass between numerous containers, undergoing multiple processes before it was dispersed into a number of storage organs, probably a repository of different nutrients.

Apparently, the zoi could transform inorganic minerals into sustenance. Like its predecessors, this zoi had descended into the solar system in the exterior part of the asteroid belt, precisely where it would find the greatest variation of minerals. We suspected that the radio signals it emitted served as a radar, enabling it to locate suitable rocks. Now, the zoi was harnessing the sunlight as fuel for what was likely a highly energy-consuming digestive process. When it later broke out of orbit, its repository would be filled with all the nutrients it needed for its onward journey.

As thoroughly as circumstances allowed, we mapped out the zoi's stationary organs as well as the movements of the mobile units. In the few months we had at our disposal, it could only amount to a rough outline of an inconceivably complex and variable system. It was a tremendous amount of work, and it was highly fascinating.

While we worked, so did the zoi. The air pockets steadily grew, and just like the previous time, they interconnected through narrow strings expanding into passageways, large enough that we were able to move through them. More air pockets formed, and we experimented with creating them ourselves, either as extensions of existing bubbles or as entirely new ones. The latter was simply done by bringing a bit of air into the fluid surrounding us. Even the tiniest bubble would quickly grow bigger, and once it was sufficiently large, we could connect it to the rest.

We still needed the space suits for navigating the rest of the zoi, but in the air-filled area, we were no longer dependent on them. And after a while, we discovered something else: We didn't experience muscle or bone loss while staying in the zoi-environment.

Usually, this is one of the major problems with space travel. Without the impact of gravity, the human body will rapidly weaken. Counteracting the deterioration takes hours of intense, daily exercise, and it was difficult to do this kind of workout inside the zoi, which was one of the reasons why the initial plan had been shifts of maximally a week's duration. When Kiah and I decided to stay for longer intervals, the doctors demanded a very thorough monitoring of the expected physical decline. But the decline failed to appear.

"That's awesome!" Kiah exclaimed when another round of tests confirmed the result. "Do you see what it means? We can stay here for months without all that tedious exercise."

"It also means that the zoi is altering our bodies," I replied. "Isn't that a bit scary?"

Kiah stretched comfortably in mid-air. "I can't see why that would be scary. The zoi has created a space in which we can live and breathe, without the suits, and now it turns out that it also prevents us from ending up as osteoporotic weaklings. I don't know about you, but I trust it means well."

Evidently, the zoi was striving to establish the optimal living conditions for us. It had even been kind enough to regulate the bioluminescence according to our circadian rhythm, periodically dimming the light to a kind of twilight. Initially, the duration of "night" and "day" fluctuated a bit, but they gradually settled into a cycle very close to twenty-four hours. It included fifteen hours of full illumination and nine hours of dimming, with a gradual transition in between.

The very fact that the zoi directly interfered with our biology felt like an unsettling prospect. Regardless of intention, it might have unforeseen consequences. But sometimes, the path to discovery will lead through unknown and incomprehensible territory. Every step in understanding the zois had required someone to take a leap, and so far, it had all gone well. Better than anyone could have imagined.

When it was time to go home, I could hardly bear the thought. Yes, I was looking forward to being out under the open sky, to seeing other people than the six I had just spent half a year with, especially Natan. But once again, this could very well be our last chance of getting to know the zois. Five of them had visited our solar system. Perhaps others had preceded them without us noticing, but it was equally likely that they were part of a group, and that at some point, this group would have passed us.

The zois had opened up the galaxy for us, demonstrating that life was out there, and that the life we had been fortunate enough to encounter wasn't hostile, but friendly and immensely hospitable. This revealed new horizons, containing possibilities we could barely fathom. Possibilities including a life in space and the interstellar travel we had otherwise been forced to give up. But it all depended on the zois. And now we were about to leave another one of them, for what might easily be the last time.

DISTANCE

We stop outside Linn's quarters. The entrance is closed. No sound can be heard from within.

"She's probably asleep," I say. "Do we have to wake her?"

I suppose I should have said *they* and *them*, but I have only seen one Linn so far, with her non-sentient shadow.

"We have to know how she's doing." Other-Amira draws herself to the opening. "Linn?" she calls out. "Are you in there?"

We wait. For a while, nothing happens, and Other-Amira calls again. Then I hear something move. The entrance partially opens, and Linn's face peeks out.

"We're here." Her voice is so faint that it's difficult to distinguish the words. "We're just... very tired."

"So, you have been separated?" I ask. "As you can see, we have too."

She nods briefly, the look on her face suggesting that whatever happened, she wouldn't have the strength to care about it. Hundreds of us could be floating out here, or we could have turned into raging monsters. She would still give the same nod.

"What can we do to help you?" Other-Amira sounds a worried as I feel. "Can we get you anything?"

"No thanks. Just let us rest."

Linn's face disappears, but the entrance remains open. Perhaps she is just too exhausted to close it, but in any case, I move closer, following Other-Amira. She is widening the entrance, enabling us both to look in.

The two of them float in there, attached to each other, but also to the wall membrane. It seems to be clinging to them. The membrane partly closes around the hip and upper body of one of the Linns. The other wriggles into the wall, as if finding a comfortable position in a bed.

"Linn?" Other-Amira hesitantly asks. "What's with the wall?"

The moving Linn takes a slow, trembling breath and looks towards us. The other one is utterly still. Asleep, I suppose.

"It takes care of us," the Linn who is awake replies. "It was hard on us. Being separated. We have very little strength. It gives us... what we need."

Other-Amira and I exchange glances.

"What do you mean?" I ask. "How can the wall give you anything?"

Another slow breath. "Don't know." The words come out in a sigh. "I feel it. Helping."

"Linn, may we come in?" Other-Amira asks, the calm of her voice sounding forced.

For some reason, the question makes my pulse race. I was inside Linn's bedchamber only yesterday. Now I have no desire at all to go in there.

"No. Stay out!" Linn pulls her upper body free from the membrane while her hips remain in place. "I mean, we'd rather be alone. I'm sorry, Amira, but I can't bear anyone coming close to me. Not right now."

Not having to enter the room is a relief. But Linn's words hurt, both because of the rejection, and because they are directed at the other me. Linn and I were so close. The shadows were no hindrance; if anything, they brought us together. But that has changed. With two independent versions of us both, it's as if there's no room for other relationships, least of all for the physical closeness that Linn and I so recently shared. Perhaps it was a kind of preparation for what we're experiencing now.

"I understand." Other-Amira sounds at once relieved and hurt, just like me. She pauses, then continues, "But I'll have to tell Evardo that you've gotten worse. And about the wall."

Linn presses her lips together, but nods at the same time.

"Do it now," she whispers. "Let's get it over with."

We wait down the passageway while the Evardos examine the two versions of Linn. One of the Evardos remains outside, receiving data from the other. The tenseness of the first Evardo's shoulders reveals how he, too, is disturbed by the proximity of other people. It must be very uncomfortable for the three inside that small room. My own urge to stay far from anyone but Amira keeps getting stronger. Even at several meters' distance the visible Evardo is too close for my liking.

After what feels like a very long time, but was probably no more than fifteen minutes, the other one emerges from the bedchamber.

"We'd better leave them in peace," he says, closing the entrance behind him.

"How bad is it?" I ask without coming any closer.

"Not good. She was already weak. The whole process has been hard on them both, but clearly hardest on one of them. She stayed unconscious throughout the examination."

"And the thing with the wall?"

Other-Amira is asking that question. The two

Evardos both hesitate, then one of them replies:

"The connection with the wall membrane is keeping them alive. Their own systems are overworked. Some of the vital organs are close to failing, and the zoi has taken over their functions."

I realize that my hand has sought Amira's. They squeeze each other tightly.

"So, they can only survive like this?" she asks. "If they leave the wall, they will die?"

"Not instantly. But they can only leave it briefly."

The thought sickens me. Linn is bound to the zoi, the creature that has ravaged her health. With the duplication, it drained the last of her strength, and now it's completely taking over both versions of her.

"Is there anything we can do?" I ask, already knowing the answer.

The Evardo who went into the bedchamber shakes his head.

"Not apart from waiting. Once she has regained her strength, she may be able to free herself."

I doubt he believes his own words. I don't. Linn will be tied to the zoi, like a dying patient confined to a hospital bed and an ever-growing array of life-supporting machines, until those machines, too, must capitulate.

"We will check on her regularly," the other Evardo adds.

"Should I—should *we* do that too?" Amira asks.

"It's probably best if you don't. At least the way

things are right now."

Amira loosens her grip on my hand, and I suppose the reverse happens too. However much I empathize with the two Linns, I'm not sure I can cope with having to seek them out. It's probably hard for the Evardos too, but they are doctors after all; professionally used to transgressing the biological boundaries of other people. Perhaps that makes it easier to overcome this sudden aversion to contact, induced by the zoi like all the other upheavals.

We could of course try to suppress that reaction, but if it's uncomfortable for everybody involved, why torment each other? After all, Linn isn't alone. There are two of her, just like there are two of Amira and me.

I realize I have started to think of her this way, not as Other-Amira, but simply Amira. Now we are two people sharing that name; two people sharing everything that until this morning was only me. I'm beginning to accept that.

One of the Evardos clears his throat.

"We will withdraw for now," he says. "If you need us, you will find us in the vicinity of our quarters. Right now, I think we all need some peace to settle into the new situation."

"You're probably right," Amira says, smiling first at him, then at me. The sight of that smile fills me with bubbling joy. It may not be such a bad thing after all to have gained a twin.

EVOLUTION

Returning home felt strange. The fourth zoi-expedition, which had been my first, was now over, and I was back on Earth. For a while I almost felt like I didn't belong there. The open spaces I had missed weren't really open but confined within Earth's atmosphere. In a way, I had been freer in space, with very little room at my immediate disposal, but surrounded by the universe itself.

Besides, I was just as restrained at the base. For the first two weeks after our return, we were confined there, partly to monitor our health, and partly to ensure that we wouldn't spread any dangerous microorganisms. We were only allowed to see our friends and family through VR- and holo-calls, and even the base personnel would wear full protection whenever we were in the same room. The only people we could interact with in a normal way were each other. In that sense, the expedition wasn't over yet.

Suddenly, I had trouble sleeping at night. It hadn't been a problem on the journey, neither during our stay in the zoi nor on our way there and back. But now that I was home again, and the planet kept both me and my blanket tied down on the mattress, I couldn't find any rest.

During the third night in a row when I lay awake well past midnight, I stood up and went outside. A garden door in my room opened out into a courtyard located within the part of base where we were in isolation. The sky above me was black and moonless, and by planetary standards, the stars stood out vividly. But still, they were blurred by the man-made light always present even here in the desert, as well as the atmospheric layers protecting the planet.

"So, you can't sleep either?"

It was Kiah's voice. She stood in the middle of the courtyard, hardly visible in the darkness.

"No," I replied, walking over to her. She looked up at the sky, and I followed her gaze.

"The same stars," she said. "Here, they seem much more distant."

I understood what she meant. We had seen the stars from space. On a cosmic scale, they weren't any further away here on Earth, but the atmosphere constituted a barrier. Out there, we had been among the stars. Here, we were merely observing them.

"What ungrateful wretches we are," I said,

laughing softly. "We have barely returned home, haven't seen our family and friends yet, and we are already yearning to leave."

"We yearn for what's truly worth yearning for. Family and friends—they're just people. There are billions of them, huddled together on one small planet. But we have encountered life in the universe. How many can make that claim?"

"Yeah, well." I did feel a bit unsettled by Kiah's remark. "That doesn't make everything else trivial."

"Not trivial, but..." Kiah turned towards me. "The encounter with the zois is crucial! For all human history, we have been trapped here on Earth, and when we finally ventured into space, all we could reach were dead rocks. Now, for the first time, we have met an alien life form, and this encounter could lead to others. It may be the most important thing that has ever happened."

The most important thing ever? Life on our own planet had to be more essential. Humanity was still learning how to maintain the conditions for our own existence rather than undermine them through excessive resource consumption. Even an honest opportunity for a space dwelling existence could never be more important than that. But I knew what Kiah meant. And on a strictly personally level, I might even agree.

We were very thoroughly examined, and the results were compared with the tests and examinations we had conducted on the journey.

Our hormonal system had evidently undergone some changes during our stay in the zoi. This applied to all participants in the expedition, but because Kiah and I had stuck out the unpleasant adaptation, the changes followed a different pattern in our case. While the others had only experienced disturbances, our systems had reached a new balance. It seemed to counteract the negative effects that prolonged exposure to weightlessness typically has on the human biological system.

The doctors weren't unconditionally pleased with this development. Manipulating the hormonal system was always a risky affair. Working from the basis of two centuries of medical research, they themselves hadn't fully mastered it. We definitely couldn't expect an alien and seemingly non-intelligent being to gain a superior expertise within a matter of weeks.

"It doesn't *have* to be intelligent," Kiah irritably told the doctor, Evardo Mendoza, who was examining us. "When our own body regulates our hormones, it's not exactly relying on intellect, is it?"

"Your body makes use of mechanisms developed

over millions of years," Evardo replied. "The zoi won't be able to imitate that in such a short time."

"It looks like it did."

"We'll see. Now, please keep completely still."

The scanner closed around Kiah's body. Obediently, she lay unmoving until all procedures were completed, and the scanner opened again.

"Well?" she stated.

"It looks like you're not getting enough sleep. Would that be a correct assessment?"

Kiah sat up. "I've been sleeping rottenly for a while," she confirmed. "But only since I returned home. It has nothing to do with the zoi."

"It could be a delayed effect." Evardo looked over at me. "Have you experienced anything similar?"

"Yes," I admitted. "I've had difficulty sleeping ever since our return. Couldn't it just be a belated, psychological reaction?"

"It's feasible, but we need to take all possibilities into account. Now, it's your turn."

Kiah stepped away from the examination table, and I took her place. The machine components connected around me, and I heard the buzzing from the scanning modules moving over my body, one by one. Then, the screens slid away again.

"The results for the two of you are completely similar," Evardo said. "You both show signs of moderate sleep deprivation, but apart from that, the conclusion remains unchanged from last time: you are unusually fit and healthy, considering that you've just returned from a space journey lasting nearly a year. The same isn't true for your colleagues. They have all lost muscle mass, and their bone density has deteriorated somewhat. In addition, they display the kind of disturbance in the circulatory and neural systems which is common in astronauts after longer periods of weightlessness. This kind of disturbance is completely absent in your scan results."

"And you see that as a problem?" Kiah let out an exasperated sigh. "The zoi has helped us. Evidently, it can read and influence our biological system with greater accuracy than we can. Why not just accept that as a fact?"

"Because there's too much we don't understand. The two of you are scientists and astronauts. As such, you are accustomed to juggling wild theories and running great personal risks. But as a doctor, my duty is to care for my patients' health in the best possible way, based on solid evidence, and I will maintain that ETLEA should exercise a reasonable degree of caution. It is not enough to simply observe that you appear to be fine. We must understand *why*."

"Amira has a theory about that," Kiah says, nodding towards me. "And she is a xenobiologist, so she knows what she's talking about. Explain it to him, Amira."

Honestly, I didn't feel like engaging in a lengthy discussion at the moment, but I couldn't ignore her request. And Evardo looked genuinely interested. He was a bit of a stickler, but he would probably listen.

"Briefly, my theory is that the zois have no immune defense system. They have the exact opposite: a system designed to ensure the survival of any foreign organism they may encounter."

Evardo raised his eyebrows. "The immune defense is essential for all forms of life. If an organism doesn't defend itself against intruders, it won't survive for long."

"On Earth, it won't." I made a gesture with my hand. "Life is everywhere here. Organisms competing for the same resources; organisms surviving by parasitic strategies. But in space, the conditions are radically different. Life exists out there, we now know as much, but it must be incredibly rare. Parasitic life forms would never develop under such conditions, as they wouldn't have anything to parasitize."

"That's true," Evardo said, nodding. "I find it hard to imagine, but I see your point. An immune defense system is very resource intensive, so if it isn't needed, it may never develop."

"Or it would change function." I was starting to warm up to the topic. "We have no idea how the zois originated, and initially, they may have lived under conditions more like ours. But they must have been space dwelling for a very long time, perhaps billions of years, and in space, their problem wouldn't have been defending themselves against other organisms.

On the contrary, any direct contact would represent an opportunity."

"For what?"

"Evolution. The zois seem to be structured like oversized single-celled organisms, and we assume they reproduce through cloning. This means they lack the capacity for change that sexual reproduction represents. But in return, single cell organisms are capable of directly exchanging genetic material and engaging in what's called an endosymbiosis: a process in which a larger cell incorporates a smaller one. As a matter of fact, the complex cells constituting our own bodies arose through an endosymbiosis. Without it, all life would still be at the bacterial stage."

Evardo frowned. "I think I heard about that in medical school. Something about one of the important organelles in a cell originally being an independent organism. The mitochondrion, perhaps?"

"Exactly," I said. "The mitochondrion still retains some of its own DNA, even though it has been a component of the eukaryote cell, the basis of all multicellular life, for something approaching two billion years. Back then, it was a small bacterium which happened to be absorbed into a larger cell. By an incredibly lucky series of events, this incident became a mutually beneficial working relationship, as the mitochondria provided their hosts with a surplus of energy, hugely expanding the possibility for evolutionary development."

"So, you think this is how the evolution of the zois take place—through assimilation of other life forms?"

"Yes, and because they so rarely encounter other life forms, they have developed a welcoming mechanism rather than a defense. All the zois we have interacted with have done the same: They quickly assess our physical needs and instantly begin to fulfill them. As soon as our immediate survival has been ensured, the mechanism starts analyzing our well-being in a long-term sense. Apparently, it recognizes the detrimental effect of weightlessness on our bodies and sets out to correct it. I have no idea how, but I'm pretty sure that's what's happening."

"It's an alluring theory," Evardo said. "But I can't believe it. It's much too improbable."

"Is it?" Kiah interjected. "I'm not a biologist, but Amira has been explaining to me how life actually functions; how insanely complex it is. Each cell operates through an abundance of finely tuned processes that we only partially understand, and in multicellular life, they take part in a collaboration which is even more unfathomable. How likely does it seem that two tiny cells joining up will grow into an entire human being? Consider all the incredibly intricate processes going on in our bodies, or for that matter, in a tree, or a mosquito, or a fungus. It's all ridiculously improbable. But still, it works."

"Even so, it's just a hypothesis." Evardo walked to

the scanner. "I will complete my analysis of today's test results and forward them to my colleagues on the medical team. Then we will try to assess when you may safely return home."

"Thank you!" Kiah said through clenched teeth. "We really appreciate that."

She marched out of the room, and I followed behind. On my way out the door, I turned my head and looked back at Evardo. He was still standing by the scanner, apparently without doing anything. Even if he had dismissed my theory, it seemed to have made an impression.

UNITY

Hand in hand, we float in front of the membrane wall in the elongated room nearest to the nucleus. Amira and Amira. I'm getting used to being two people.

Out in the cytosol, a large arachnid swims past us, heading for the nucleus. The name derives from the long limbs, eight in total, characterizing this kind of organelle. They move between the nucleus and various other parts of the zoi, transferring some kind of information.

Amira giggles.

"Sorry," she says when I send her a surprised look. "This image just popped into my head, of you and me as a newly in love couple at a holographic show or at the theater." She blushes, and I feel myself doing the same. "I mean, not because I think we are," she continues. "In love, that is. But I guess you know that."

"Yes," I reply. "I know what you're feeling. Or at least, I think I do."

An awkward silence ensues. I'm pretty certain that we're both contemplating how paradoxical it appears that we feel this flustered around someone who is essentially ourselves, or at least very recently was. In a way it's the opposite of falling in love and having another person seem like a part of yourself.

"This is exactly what I longed for as a child," I continue. "Someone who truly understood me—apart from Karim, of course, but he was so much older."

The look Amira gives me makes me realize what I've said. This leads right back to the argument about who is the original and who is the copy. But she reads my reaction just as easily and anticipates my apology:

"It's okay," she says. "It's just as hard for me to grasp that we are two people with exactly the same memories." She ponders for a moment. "Perhaps we should only use the word *I* in reference to the time following our separation. Before that, it's *we*. We were both there, even if there was only one of us."

I nod. "It may feel a little strange, but you're right. That's the kind of thing we will have to do."

Once again, we fall silent while observing the spectacle unfolding around us. The organelles move about in a grand choreography, never in the way of each other, never dubious about their tasks. I recall my old enchantment with their dance, the faith I used to have in the zoi.

"Now, we're two," Amira says after a while. "Which leaves us with the question: Are we still the same person?"

We turn in the air. I let go of her hand, and we hang there facing each other as if looking into a mirror. It's the same facial features I'm watching, the same body, but she doesn't mirror my movements. It's profoundly disturbing. My reflection suddenly turning into an autonomous creature, that's a common horror trope. I'm not scared of Amira, not in the sense that I suspect she means me harm. But still, I'm on shaky ground.

"We're not the same," I reply. "At least, not entirely."

"No. Not entirely."

She raises a hand in front of her. I copy the motion, and the palms of our hands meet, just as they would on the surface of a mirror. As no gravity anchors us, the touch pushes both of us backwards in opposite directions. Just a few meters, but it's enough to make my heart beat faster. My stomach drops.

"Amira!"

I'm not sure which one of us cried out. Nor how we turn back towards each other, but we do. Moments later, I have her in a tight grasp.

"Why do we feel like this?" she gasps. "It's so... intense. If we're separated by even a small distance, it's like stepping straight into an abyss."

"The zoi," I reply, "It controls us. Our emotions. Our actions."

"Yes, but why does it want to keep us together? And for that matter, why does it keep us away from the others?"

"I don't know, but I don't like being manipulated like that."

Without letting go of my hands, she lets herself slide back slightly. "Maybe it's just some kind of transitional stage. It's possible we haven't completed the process of becoming separate beings. In that case, it will probably pass."

"And then it's followed by something else!" I exclaim. "Another change which might be even more radical. You said it yourself when we spoke with the others: It's turning us into a part of its organism, in a way we won't necessarily like."

"I did say that." Her gaze follows a couple of arachnids heading towards an opening into the nucleus. "But the more I think about it... We hardly have a choice. Whether we want it or not, we will become part of the zoi. But we could have some influence over *how* it happens, if we try to shape the process rather than just fight it."

My insides turn cold. "You sound like Kiah."

"And what if I do?" Amira meets my gaze, looking resolute and a little nervous. "In fact, I'm starting to think that we haven't been entirely fair to Kiah. We've felt betrayed by her, but perhaps we share some of the blame for drifting apart because we've been so dismissive of everything she said."

If there's a truth to that, I don't want to hear it. I'm tired of Kiah. She has let me down, and now Amira does too by defending her. I pull my hands away, turn my back on her and kick off. It should be possible, *must* be possible. I am myself, not her, nor the zoi.

For a second or two, nothing happens. Then the separation anxiety hits me with full intensity: cold sweat, pounding heart, buzzing ears. I try to resist, but my vision blurs, and I feel dizzy, unable to sense where I am. With trembling hands, I seek out the wall and push off, back in the direction where I know she is. It's the only thing I know for certain.

The anxiety only eases slowly. Even when I feel her skin against mine, my heart is still acting like a fluttering moth. Her arms grab me with a desperate clumsiness, and I grab back at her.

"Damn it, Amira," she whispers in my ear. "Why did you do that?"

"I'm sorry, Amira."

For a while, we just float there, in a tight embrace that gradually loosens itself. My vision has cleared, and I see that she's crying.

"You'd think it was the easiest thing in the world, right? Talking to yourself."

I smile, shaking my head. "Apparently not."

My anger has drowned in other emotions. Her

hand seeks mine, and I caress it. She lets out a little relieved sob and attempts to wipe the shield of tears from her eyes. Water bubbles float out into the room.

"I hate it," she says. "Crying in this place. But of course, you know that."

"Yes. I know all about that."

She rubs her eyes again. With a few blinks, she seems to have expelled the tears. "We are clearly not the same person. How did we become so different in such a short time?"

"Perhaps we didn't," I say, stroking her still wet cheek. "Perhaps we have just chosen different sides in an internal struggle we have had for a while. That's probably why I reacted like that."

"Please don't do it again, no matter how angry you get." She smiles, but she's serious too. Neither of us can endure this kind of reaction. We need to stay together, that's a condition we will have to accept, like we must accept everything else the zoi is doing to us. Exactly as she just said.

I return her smile. "Don't worry. I won't."

"Maybe we should discuss it with the others. Hear their opinion about what's going on. Kiah's too."

It doesn't sound very convincing. Her aversion to the very idea of approaching anyone but me, probably mirrors my own feelings. Being with Amira, and only Amira, is all I can cope with.

"At some point we should do that," I reply. "But not right now."

Once again, I meet her gaze, and in that moment, it's like looking into a mirror. There's no reservation, no fear of how the other will react.

"You're right," she mumbles. "Not right now."

Nothing should disturb our unity; this feeling is so powerful that I think I might be sensing it from both of us. I have found myself in someone else, someone else in me. My life before her seems sad and lonely, no matter how many people I surrounded myself with. They could never be anything but strangers. Amira and I may disagree on specific things, but it will always be based on something I understand. As long as I have her, why would I need anyone else?

PROCREATION

A month had passed before we were finally let out. Of course, I had spoken to Natan on the holo several times a day, but seeing him again, feeling his beard against my cheek, his arms around me—at that moment I was truly home, with him, back on Earth. Right then, I wanted nothing more.

I was under strict orders to take at least six months' leave from ETLEA. During that time, I traveled with Natan for a couple of projects he was participating in. The first had to do with preserving the Namibian steppe fauna, and the second was an investigation of the ecosystems in some remaining parts of the Amazon rainforest. When he finished that, we'd visit first my family, then his.

The Namibian savannah could hardly be more different from the zoi environment—vast, open, and dry. In many places, it was turning into a desert, which was the focus of the effort. Natan had no prior experience with prevention of desertification, but as always, he was quickly captured by the new subject.

My half-hearted attempts to contribute didn't amount to much. Natan and I agreed this was completely fair. I had been hard at work 24/7 for almost a year. Naturally, I needed some time to simply relax.

Most of the time, I remained in the tent. Outside, I would quickly start feeling dizzy and nauseous. Not seriously so, but enough that I avoided venturing too far into the terrain. I told Natan that this was due to the heat, combined with an overall fatigue, but I was a bit worried myself. Was I developing agoraphobia?

I felt better in the Amazonas. The rainforest was humid, dense, and teeming with life. To my relief, as well as Natan's, I started to perk up a bit, despite the suffocating heat. I helped gathering data on the chemical intercommunication between the various life forms in the forest. In this ancient and highly complex biological system, countless connections bound plants, fungal networks, microbes, insects, and all the larger animal species together, forming a vast superorganism. Not unlike the zoi, but on a much larger scale.

And then the family visits began. I had been entirely content with leaving them for last, as my relationship with my parents had become rather strained. They hadn't exactly been thrilled when I was hired by ETLEA, and even less when I was chosen for the zoi expedition.

My father had cried when I told him over the holo. "You're our only child. We hardly ever see you, and now you're leaving the planet for a whole year. What if something happens to you?"

"Things could happen anywhere," I had replied in a voice sounding harsh even to myself. "Do you want me to wrap myself in cotton wool for your peace of mind? I have my own life to live."

At that point, this was the end of the discussion. There was no way I would withdraw from the crew, and they knew that. But now I had to spend a couple of weeks in their company, with no signed mission contract to hold up as a shield in front of me.

The first couple of days went by without incident. They were all happy to see me—my mother and father, grandparents, aunts, uncles, and cousins. Most of them still lived in the same town, and none of them had left the country for more than a short vacation, except for Karim. At the moment, he was in Svalbard, but he would return home for a visit in a week's time.

On the fourth day, we were invited to dinner at my maternal grandparents' house. My uncle Latif and his family were present too, including my cousin Hasna and her two children aged two and five.

"You're so lucky," my mother told Latif and his wife, Farida. "Two lovely grandchildren." She watched the two children tumbling around on the floor with their father. The longing in her gaze hit me harder than any sarcastic remark could have.

"Hasna is four years older than Amira," Farida said. "She still has plenty of time."

She smiled at me, apparently unaware of how touchy the subject was. This only made me angrier.

"I'm not planning to have children," I curtly replied.

Farida shook her head, still smiling. "Wait and see, you'll probably change your mind. But don't wait too long. It's getting harder with age, you know."

"I'm aware of that, thank you. But I won't change my mind. Besides, that's my business—not something anyone else should meddle in."

"Wouldn't Natan have a say in the matter?"

I deliberately avoided looking at Natan.

"Not over whether Amira wants children," I heard him reply. "That's entirely her own decision."

"Do you want them?" Farida asked him.

"Whether I do or not, it isn't something we should discuss here."

"But it's not that simple," Farida persisted. "Children don't just belong to their parents. Your mother and father, Amira, they want grandchildren. Will you deny them this joy?"

I faced my mother. Had she orchestrated this? Surely, she had complained to her brother and sister-in-law. Perhaps she had even asked Farida to nag me. Mother just turned away. For whatever reason, she couldn't meet my gaze.

"I'm not denying them anything! I'm sure lots of children out there need grandparents. Go find some of them. It can't be that hard."

"Amira, family is family. And you're an only child, that carries an obligation."

That was enough! I stood up, forcefully pushing the chair against the table.

"I have no obligations whatsoever! I have gone into space, and all you can think about is whether I'll procreate. I'm going to bed now. Goodnight."

I could hear Natan following me, but it wasn't until we were walking down the street towards my parents' house that he caught up to me. He didn't say anything. We continued walking for a while, then I burst out.

"Why does it have to be like that? They don't care about what I have achieved. I'm just a birthing machine refusing to work."

Natan stayed silent. Wise of him, but he knew me well. Letting me do the thinking myself was the best strategy in a situation like this.

"Okay, it's not that bad, I know. But it's like they don't understand that you could want anything from life except from family life and job security. They keep pestering Karim too, just not about children. But then, he isn't an only child." I sighed and wiped the tears of anger, which were now thankfully retreating, from the corners of my eyes. "I can't wait to see him."

"Do you know when he'll be arriving?" Natan asked.

"In three days, if his travels go according to plan." We both remained silent for a few seconds, then I said, "Natan, the thing about children... we agree about that, don't we?"

"Are you sure this is a good time to discuss it?"

I laughed. "Because I'm pissed off? Don't worry, I have calmed down by now."

He looked at me with a hint of ironic doubt in his eyes. "Really?"

"Really. And to a certain extent, Farida is right— it's not a question we can just ignore. Either we agree on it, or..." I shrugged. "Well, then I'm honestly not sure what to do. *Do* you want children?"

I felt so sure he would say no. Natan cherished his freedom too, all his various projects.

"Yes," he replied. "I do."

My legs stalled. Natan stopped too, and I stared at him, mouth gaping, like stupid fish. Then I managed to pick up my jaw and ask:

"But... what should we do, then?"

He put his hands in his pockets. "Well, that depends on exactly what you're averse to. Is it just about your work?"

I had never thought that far. Children simply weren't a part of my plans for the future.

"Not just that," I replied after some thought. "If you are considering the possibility that I could bear them, and you could take care of them, then no—I don't want to do that."

"I didn't expect you to." He smiled wryly. "Too bad I can't manage that part. But we could find someone else to take care of it."

"A surrogate mother?"

"That's one option. But what I actually had in mind was finding someone who wants to form a family with us. Maybe a group of people."

"Oh."

I had no idea what to say. The whole idea was too new, with too many overwhelming possibilities. It would be so much easier if he felt the same way I did. But I had as little right to dictate his desires as he had to dictate mine.

We started walking again.

"I understand if you need to think about it," he said. "You don't have to make a decision right away. But at some point, we need to discuss it again. Then we'll see if we can find a solution."

CONTROL

The room overlooking the nucleus of the zoi has become our favorite place. Each day, Amira and I head there immediately after waking up and stay for most of the day. Observing life within the zoi is more than a pastime. In fact, it's our primary duty as xenobiologists: studying our host as a biological creature, striving to comprehend the workings of its organism. I—we—have neglected this task for too long, but now we're sharing the workload. In more ways than one, that makes it easier.

Now and then, we spot the others at a distance; pairs of doubles like us, always close to each other. We haven't spoken to any of them since the day of separation, which was more than one week ago. Keeping to ourselves in such a confined space with limited facilities presents some logistical challenges. But so far, we have been able to overcome them.

Today, we have been at work for a couple of hours. We haven't eaten yet, and I'm starting to feel hungry. I make my way over to the bag of zoi-food fastened to the wall by a string, open the bag and break off a lump. The mushy substance has formed a dry crust, and when I bring it up to my nose, it smells slightly stale.

"Has it gone bad?" Amira asks from behind me.

I hand her the lump. "What do you think?"

She sniffs it at takes a small bite.

"I think it's edible. But we'd better go fetch a fresh batch."

Normally, we simply pluck the foodstuff directly from the pantry wall, and we have no way of cooling it or keeping it fresh by other means. There's no reason to do so as the zoi constantly produces new nourishment for us—and if it stopped doing that, we'd be screwed anyway. When we keep this stockpile in the bag, it's to avoid too many trips to the pantry. Every time we go in, we run the risk of encountering some of the others.

I break off another lump, smell it and start chewing. The nondescript, porridge-like flavor has turned slightly sour, which is almost an improvement. Perhaps we should start experimenting with maturing and fermenting it, even though it's objectively unnecessary. The food is always there, completely fresh and compiled of precisely the nutrients we need. But it's unbelievably dull.

"I need to use the toilet too," Amira says. "Can we do it now?"

Visits to the lavatory present yet another practical problem. We have become adept at holding it, but there's a limit to how much we can draw it out. Every so often we simply have to go.

"Okay."

We navigate the passageways. Thankfully, there's no one in the living room, but when we approach the lavatory, I see a person floating outside. A Kiah. She's probably standing guard while her twin is using the facilities, to avoid a sudden encounter with other crew members. She looks up and spots Amira and me just as we both pause our movement with a hand to the wall.

For a split second, my emotions shift. I feel an urge to continue towards her, to be with someone other than Amira, perhaps even a specific desire to speak to Kiah. Her alienness pales in comparison with the changes I myself have undergone. We have both become two people, and we have had to learn to cope with that situation. Something in Kiah's gaze tells me this has not been unproblematic, even for her.

Then the need for distance takes over. Amira and I push ourselves backwards, and we wait in the living room until the two Kiahs come out of the opening leading to the lavatory. As they pass through the room, one of them sends me a little smile, but she doesn't say anything. A pulling sensation tells me Amira is already heading towards the opening.

"Come on!" she pleads in the slightly desperate tone of someone in urgent need of relieving themselves, and I follow her.

Now, I'm the one floating outside, waiting for Amira to finish. Being in separate rooms is a strain, even though the distance is minimal. But I need to keep watch, for everybody's sake. If another couple walked in on us by mistake, it would be equally unpleasant for all of us.

She comes out, and we switch places. While using the toilet, I catch myself wondering if this could be done some other way, without the seat and the vacuum tube. Not just a new piece of BB-tech made from synthesized zoi materials, but a solution fully integrated with the zoi. We could begin with studying how it handles waste products from the organelles...

I break off the line of thought. It leads directly towards the aquarium; adapting to living in liquid like the organelles do. Maybe even further than that, towards a fundamental alteration of our digestive system. Even absent-mindedly contemplating the possibility is dangerously close to accepting my fate.

I conclude my use of the toilet with a rinse, wipe myself and thoroughly clean my hands. Presumably, these kinds of hygienic precautions have little practical significance. The zoi is regulating our microbiome too, and while some of the gut bacteria used to present a danger if introduced into the wrong end of the digestive system, they now appear to be completely harmless to us. But still, the mere thought of being indifferent to them fills me with disgust, accompanied by an existential dread of dissolving the boundary between inside and outside, between me and not-me.

"What's wrong, Amira? You look completely off."

Amira looks at me worriedly when I exit the lavatory. I shake my head.

"It's nothing. Let's go back."

She takes my hand. "You have been preoccupied all morning. Please tell me what's bothering you."

I'm about to give another dismissive answer. But I mustn't push her away. Out mutual bond is the most important thing in the world. In a way, it's all I have.

"I will," I say. "But not here."

We have a long talk, back in the room near the nucleus. Both of us say things I have hardly dared think, about our life in the zoi, both now and in the future.

"Do you regret coming here?" she asks.

I force myself to consider the question.

"No," I reply. "I still want this; traveling with the zoi out into the universe. Getting to know it more deeply than a single year's stay will allow. But it frightens me to have so little control, not just over the zoi, but over myself."

She grimaces. "I know. All these hormone-induced emotions dictating my actions. Am I still myself, or am I really the zoi?"

"That's how I felt about Kiah all along," I exclaim. "She just accepted it all without any kind of resistance. How could she do that and remain the same person? Was she even still human?"

"I think she reacted exactly like herself, in accordance with her personality and history. And that look the two of you exchanged today..." Amira pauses for a moment. "Maybe you're beginning to reconnect. Or we are. I don't know."

She bites her lip. Now she is the one being scared by her own thoughts. I put my arms around her.

"Nothing can replace what you and I have," I declare. "I may regain my friendship with Kiah, or with Linn, if she makes it. But having you... it's a kind of connection I've never felt before. Not even with Natan."

"The same to you," she whispers. "But I have a feeling that it won't last. We will lose each other again."

"How would that even happen? We can't get that far away from each other here in the zoi. With time, our need to stay close together may disappear. But that doesn't mean we'll be separated."

"We don't know that! Perhaps we will get the opposite urge. An aversion to being together." She withdraws from my embrace and looks into my eyes. "And if this urge is just as powerful, we can't do anything about it."

"It's all speculation." My tone of voice is intended

to reassure us both. "We don't know what is going to happen."

"Don't we?"

Her gaze indicates a thought that almost reaches me, directly, through our eyes and into my brain. Then it's gone.

"I don't," I firmly state. "If you understand something that escapes me, please enlighten me."

But Amira shakes her head. "You're right. We don't know anything. I suppose that's what we must learn to live with. The lack of control."

I nod, considering the matter for a while.

"Maybe we could regain some influence over what happens to us by facing it head-on. The way we've handled things so far certainly hasn't helped."

We are probably thinking the same thing: that both repression and acceptance are governed by the zoi. Do we have any choice at all in how we react? I'm not sure. But behaving as if we do is probably the best course of action.

FAMILY

Everyone in the family pretended that the argument between Farida and me had never taken place, but that didn't prevent the atmosphere from becoming increasingly tense. To a certain extent, this was my fault, as I kept feeling angry about the way they interfered in my personal choices and how little they appreciated what I had achieved. I was a goddamn astronaut, one of the very few people who had encountered an actual space alien, but in their eyes, that didn't seem to count.

Things lightened up a bit when Karim returned home. Now, at least there was one person who wanted to hear about my experiences, and who had exciting stories of his own to tell. This made it easier to interact with the rest of the family, although it didn't resolve anything. Not in relation to Natan either. He spoke no more about having children, but the question still lingered between us, even as we moved on to his family.

Family, in this case, was a rather broad term. Natan's parents had never shared a household, but they had lived in the same neighborhoods and always remained on good terms. His mother had a fair number of partners in the past, but never moved in with any of them. She had an older child from a former relationship, Natan's half-brother who was eight years his senior, and while Natan's father never had any other children of his own, twenty years prior, he married a man whose daughters Natan considered his sisters. Some of these half- and step-siblings were themselves part of alternative family constellations.

One of the first days, we visited his sister Hanna, who had formed a four-parent family together with her girlfriend Imani and a male couple. Hanna had given birth to one of their children, and Imani to the two others. The four of them had stuck together for more than ten years, and they seemed to be very happy together.

"That's another way to do it," Natan said when we were back in his mother's guest room.

"Do what?" I asked, even though I knew exactly what he meant.

"Have a family. It may contain more than one father and mother."

"Of course it may. But I'm not sure if that changes anything. They all want to be parents. I don't."

Natan looked away. "Strictly speaking, you don't have to," he said after a while. "I mean, if I found someone to have those children with, you could still be my partner. Stay with us when you're not working. Wouldn't that be a possibility?"

I thought about it for a long time before I responded, trying to imagine what it would be like. After all, I spend most of my time away from home. Was the character of that home even that important?

"I don't know," I said at last.

"Consider it for a while, then we'll discuss it again."

Natan's smile was slightly strained. I felt pressured, even though he hadn't tried to talk me into anything. It was difficult to offer counterarguments, but it felt like a saddening prospect; orbiting a family I wasn't really part of, like some kind of satellite. It was not how I wanted to live my life. But this was evidently important to Natan. How could we solve that problem?

My leave ended, and I started working again. Usually, this made me forget everything else, but for the first time, I had a hard time focusing on the tasks ahead. My thoughts kept drifting off in other directions, and

I zoned out in front of the papers or my computer.

Kiah and I shared an office. Here, we were meant to collaborate in processing and interpreting the results from the expedition. I wished I could have had a room to myself, but I tried not to let Kiah sense it. Of course, I failed. After a few days had passed, she came over and sat down in front of me.

"Well," she said, crossing her arms over her chest, "what's wrong?"

I shrugged, still facing my computer. "I'm just thinking about something. Personal matters."

I hoped that would deter her. We had seldom discussed our lives outside of ETLEA. But she kept looking at me expectantly, and I continued:

"Natan and I disagree about something, and it's been weighing on my mind. That's all."

"Does he want children?"

I slammed the screen shut. "Are you reading my mind, or what?"

"A qualified guess." She smiled wryly. "I am a psychologist, after all."

I found myself explaining the whole dilemma to her. Really, it was a relief. I hadn't talked about it before, not to anyone from my own family, of course, but neither to someone from Natan's or any of our mutual friends. I was too afraid of their response. But with Kiah, it was quite another matter.

"That's a really shitty situation," she said. "You love him, don't you?"

"Yes. And I love the life that we have together. I don't want it to change."

"But it will. Radically. Children turn everything upside down. People often delude themselves that it's something they will be in control of. But you can't control a damn thing."

I didn't understand. It sounded like she spoke from personal experience.

"You don't have any children, do you?"

"No. But I used to have one."

She stared into the air for a while. I didn't dare to speak, just waited for her to continue.

"A little boy," she finally said. "Sefu. I had him for four months. Then he died."

"How?" I ventured to ask.

"Crib death." She shrugged. "*Sudden infant death syndrome*, that's the operative term for a child suddenly ceasing to breathe, without any apparent reason. Up to that point, he had been completely healthy. One day, he just didn't wake up."

"Kiah..." I reached out a hand towards her, in the kind of awkward gesture you make when you have no idea what to do or say. With a slight smile, she let me touch her arm; placed her hand over mine.

"It was a long time ago. I have learned to live with it. In any case, we're not talking about me right now, but about you and Natan. Whether you are going to have a child together, or if he's having one independently—and what you are going to do in that case."

"Yes." I withdrew my hand again. "What should I do?"

"I can't tell you that. What I can tell you, is that if a child comes into the picture, it changes everything. If you stay with Natan, that child becomes part of your life. Not to mention the other way around."

"But I'll be away so much of the time! For weeks and months at a time, even years if I'm chosen for another zoi-expedition. Is that a fair thing to impose on a child?"

"That's the wrong question," Kiah said dryly. "What you need to decide is whether you can live with that situation. How you feel about being away for months or years, and then come back to a close-knit unit. It may work. Natan is clearly willing to give it a try. Are you?"

Was I? It was hard to see the rational arguments against it, but still, it was clear that I'd prefer not to. Perhaps that was enough of an answer.

EMBRACE

I wake up before she does. Amira hovers next to me, wrapped in the sleeping bag that keeps her body in place. While the shadow grew, I stopped using the bag. Even at first, when it had room enough for both me and the slender, jelly-like figure, I was too repulsed by the thought of being cramped inside a small pouch with it. I preferred to float around freely in the bedchamber.

In the initial phase of mine and Amira's mutual existence, we would continue to sleep like that. We didn't mind our naked limbs getting tangled during the night, perhaps because we were still so close to being one entity. But then it started to annoy us both, and we brought out the sleeping bags. Luckily, I had a spare one in stock.

I watch her in her sleep, the face which almost, but not quite, is my own. I think about my encounter with Kiah in the passageway outside the lavatory. A couple of days have gone by, and I haven't seen her since.

Amira shifts in the air. I reckon she's about to wake up; we usually do so almost simultaneously. But after a few grunts she resumes her slow, regular breathing. She is still deeply asleep while I lie here, wide awake. The dampened night light from the walls has long since grown into the brightness of day. Restlessly, I stir within my bag, but the bedchamber has very little room for movement, and I don't want to wake her up. Apparently, she still needs sleep, while I feel like getting up.

I wriggle out of my own sleeping bag. Just for the sake of experimentation, I move towards the exit, unlock the closing mechanism and poke my head outside. The expected anxiety fails to appear, but then our feet are still almost touching. I continue forward, through the opening. The acceptable distance between us has increased lately, so maybe staying right outside the bedchamber will be possible. Out there, I can wait for her to wake up.

Still no discomfort, even as I close the opening behind me. I should just remain here, but I can't resist exploring the limits of how far away I'm able to go. If I move slowly, I will sense the pull while it's still too weak to wake her up. With a hand on the wall membrane, I push myself forward a short distance down the passageway. Then a little further.

My heart is beating steadily. I breathe freely, without any hint of the choking sensation that would normally be the inevitable result of venturing too far away from my twin. Now, there's at least five meters between us, and it doesn't seem to be a problem.

A rush of freedom fills me as I continue down the passageway, in the direction of the living room. The bond that forced us to stay together has been broken. For the first time in so long, I can be on my own.

Will I also be able to approach the others? There's only one way to find out.

As I reach the point where the passageway bends, I stop and look back. The entrance to the bedchamber is still closed. If Amira felt my absence, she would long since have woken up and rushed out to find me. Of course, she might still feel worried if she wakes up and finds me gone. But even if that happens, she will manage. She doesn't need to be taken care of.

This makes me think about Linn. How might she —or they—be doing? I haven't looked in on them since the day of separation, and I can only hope, either that they have made it on their own, or that the Evardos have occasionally overcome their zoi-induced reactions to make sure that they were doing okay.

Linn. Worries seeps out of the secluded corner of my mind where I have shut them in. How long has it been? More than a week, maybe even two. Far too long. Linn was severely weakened the last time I saw her. She could easily have gotten worse. She might even be dead.

How could I just forget about her? I can't even call it an oversight. All the time, I have been aware that she was there in her bedchamber. That she may have lacked the strength to endure the duplication, while my own had been essentially unproblematic but still demanded my full attention.

Now, for the first time, I'm able to lift my gaze. I'd better turn it toward Linn.

The living room is empty. Moving through it, I sense that something about it has changed. It has grown slightly larger, and besides... yes, there's an additional entrance hole. Did it appear overnight? At least, I didn't notice it yesterday, when we passed through the room on our way to the lavatory.

It takes me a moment to ascertain which opening is the new one. Fortunately, the room is oblong and there are a few structures I can use as landmarks. The extra opening is on my right side, which ought to mean that the passageway leading to Linn's quarters is still the third one to the left. I'll visit her first, and afterwards, I'll figure out where the new passageway may be leading.

Occasionally, new air pockets will spontaneously

form in the cytosol and connect to the rest of the system. It mostly happened in the early phases of our habitation, while the zoi was still working on filling our basic needs. The lavatory room developed in that manner around a strategically deposited stool sample, while the pantry materialized at the opposite end of the habitat. A few of the other rooms appeared in a similar way. Now another one has apparently emerged.

The change unsettles me. The newly formed room might be filled with liquid rather than air. If such a development starts, I'll have no way of stopping it. For that very reason, dwelling on my fear of it won't do any good. Besides, I should hurry to Linn.

I'm not the only one seeking her out. The entrance to her bedchamber is open, and I hear a man's voice coming through it. Evardo's, of course. I peep inside and spot him—one of him, with two of Linn. At least, I see two versions of her body, but only one seems to be awake. Though this was also the case last time I saw them, there's a difference. The sleeping Linn is unusually pale, even for a Scandinavian, and she looks shriveled, like a dried-out plant. She is fully attached to the wall membrane. Adorning it like some kind of ornamental relief.

The other Linn, the one who is awake, also rests against the wall. She must be stuck to it, or she would float away. She, too, is pale, but not unnaturally so.

Thin, but not withered. She still looks like a living human. Her twin doesn't, at least not fully so. Maybe half of each—half alive, half human.

Evardo looks up.

"Amira. I'm glad you're here."

His smile and tone of voice remind me of the nurse who received me at the hospital, back when my grandmother lay dying. Perhaps it's a manner you develop when working professionally at the boundary between life and death. You need to convey so much in a few words and a glance. Precisely the right amount of sympathy. Acknowledgement of how terrible this is for the person you're speaking to, but also a conveyance that, right now, this is a given situation all parties will have to accept, and you need to focus on what matters most: saying goodbye and easing the dying person's last days, hours, or minutes. Soothing their pain and anxiety as much as possible.

Are we now talking days, hours, or minutes for Linn?

"I shouldn't have stayed away for so long. I'm sorry, Linn."

She turns her face towards me in a slow movement. "It's okay, Amira. You haven't been able to come until now."

Her voice is weak, though less strained than last time. She has come to terms with the situation. In a way, this is much worse than if she was still fighting it, even if that fight would consume the last of her strength. My insides clench with a grief and self-reproach I will have to keep at bay. Linn shouldn't need to feel sorry for me.

"And it's only now that I'm able to invite you in," she continues, extending her arm toward me.

Can I do it? Keeping my distance from others has become a reflex. But the thought of entering the room evokes no discomfort. It feels like I've been frozen and now I'm thawing. It's a feeling I recognize from similar situations, being reunited with someone I care about, after having been separated for a long time. It has only been a couple of weeks, but I sense that Linn has a very limited time left. I have missed a significant part of that time.

I push myself through the opening, to the side of the Linn who is awake. Freeing her upper body from the wall, she reaches out for me. Very cautiously, I embrace her. Her arms are awfully thin, her chest sunken. Tall, athletic Linn. She has become so small—though she's a lot bigger than the other Linn. While we're embracing, I give her a sidelong glance. Then I gather the courage to ask:

"What about her?"

Linn and I let go of each other, and she turns towards her shrunken twin. Their resemblance is still evident, and so is the tenderness in Linn's gaze as she touches the figure in the wall.

"She has only been conscious for short periods of time, and it hasn't happened for a while. Apparently, she's even weaker than me." Linn smiles sadly. "Neither of us will make it, at least not in the same way as the rest of you."

"In what way, then?" A mixture of hope and dread causes my voice to crack. I fear that the answer is what I see before me. A tiny body slowly sinking into the wall.

"The zoi is able to keep us alive, but the more it assists us, the more we become part of it. I can no longer leave this place. And she—" Linn nods towards her twin, "—she's hardly a separate person anymore."

"Linn." I try to keep my voice under control. "Will you be... immersed in the zoi? Like her?"

"Yes," she answers with a calmness I can hardly bear. "It will continue to envelop me. The boundary between it and me will gradually vanish. It has already begun to happen."

"What do you mean? Are you saying there is a mental connection between you and the zoi?"

"In a way. But probably not the kind you are thinking of." Linn frowns. "How can I explain it? I sense the zoi, like I sense my own body. That doesn't mean I understand what's going on inside it. And right now, the sensation is very faint, because I'm trying to be the Linn that you know."

In that moment, our eyes meet, and a twinge of fear shoots through me, the dread of the borderland between the familiar and the strange. *Unheimlich.* This is Linn, and simultaneously it's something other than her. This other will gradually become predominant, until she resembles the little figure in the wall.

"It scared me at first," Linn continues. "But I have begun to accept it, and now it feels almost... comforting. The zoi welcomes me. Finally, I have found my place within it, after such a long struggle between its system and mine. We're no longer fighting. We're becoming one."

I want to protest, but what can I say? With a jerk, I turn towards Evardo. He has to be able to do something, stop it from happening. But he just nods, slowly and solemnly.

"It's for the best. Even before all this happened, I wasn't sure how long Linn would endure. I can admit that now."

Linn reaches out and squeezes his hand.

"You did your very best, Evardo, I'm grateful for that. But it's been so tough. I have felt so miserable. And now, it's over."

I should be happy for her, or at least I should accept the situation like she does herself, and like Evardo does, because he sees no better alternative. Linn isn't going to adapt. One version of her simply isn't viable, and disconnected from the zoi, the other twin would soon perish as well. Then her body would still be engulfed, unless we threw it out into space. The zoi consumes our waste products, absorbs them as nutrition, while also extracting information about us and our needs. Doing this in another way, even before the two Linns have ended their life, must provide it with even more data. It's undoubtedly rational—in a sense, it's beautiful. But at the same time, it's revolting, and it has implications I'm afraid to think through. Implications for the other three, or rather six of us. What will ultimately happen to us?

Linn yawns. Her eyelids flutter, like she's struggling to keep her eyes open.

"Oh, Amira," she murmurs, reaching out for me once more. "Don't be sad. Everything's fine. I'm just tired now."

I force myself to embrace her again, hoping she won't sense my hesitation. But she's already drifting into sleep, oblivious to everything but the organism that is welcoming her. Nourishing her body. Granting her peace.

CHOICES

Making the final decision took a long time, first for me, and then for Natan. For months, I weighed the pros and cons, even though I kept ending up with the same result: I did not want to have children, and I couldn't expect Natan to split his life in two. I had to give him either a yes or a no, and it would have to be no.

Neither of us wanted to leave the other. We stayed together for a while longer, but it was a relationship in limbo. When Natan announced that he was moving out, it was a relief. I had dreaded the moment when he had left, when I was alone in the apartment, perhaps regretting my decision. I had imagined that it would hurt too much to see him when he was no longer my partner; that I would have to lose him completely. But when he called me a few weeks later, asking if I wanted to meet up, I realized that I did. He was still my friend.

In any case, I didn't have much time to sit by myself in the apartment. At ETLEA, we were working at full throttle, preparing the next expedition, while still trying to squeeze as much as possible out of the data brought home from the previous one. My own contribution to this was outlining the differences and similarities between zoi biology and its earthly equivalent. The results of this comparison made me increasingly convinced that we were genetically related. The basic construction that we shared, a simple, fluid-filled cell containing a DNA-based genome, had at some point in Earth's early history arrived from space, and from this seed, all other life forms had developed, from the tiniest bacteria to the largest mammals.

Somewhere else in space, evolution had occurred under very different conditions, resulting in the zois. But as for how it had happened, I was still miles away from a conclusion. Did they start out as space-dwelling beings, or had their initial development taken place on a planet or another type of celestial body? It was impossible to say for sure. Precisely because the zois travelled freely in empty space, we lacked the kind of information found in Earth's geology: the remains of archaic life forms and the traces of violent events or gradual changes in the environment.

All we had, were the zois themselves, and we only

had access to them for a limited time, with years in between. Just like the two previous expeditions, the one I attended had left devices in the zoi that were meant to continue our research and project the resulting data back to Earth. However, none of them lasted for long. This time, we had chosen purely biology-based equipment, which during every expedition had proved more durable in the zoi environment—but it made a minor difference at the most. The devices worked for a couple of weeks, then they, too, started sending error messages, and shortly after, they fell silent.

Our opportunities for studying the zois were thus severely limited. When one of them appeared, we had a window determined by their migratory pattern and the practical challenges of space travel. During our last expedition, we had managed to stay in the zoi for four months. We tried our best to extend the timeframe for next expedition, but even with the most meticulous planning, there were limits to how long it could last. In any case, these finite stays could only provide us with direct insights into a specific part of the zois' life cycle. Under those circumstances, how would we ever hope to truly understand them?

I developed a habit of staring into the night sky. This was the same sky that had arched over me throughout my entire life. In principle, I had always been aware that it represented a universe in which our planet was no more than a random dot. But now I had experienced it firsthand, through my own senses. To me, the sky would never again appear as the light-studded shell seeming to form an upper boundary of my world. It was an opening into infinity. The weight of the planet kept me grounded, but I knew that it was possible to break free.

For a long while, I heard nothing from Natan about any concrete family plans. But one day, roughly six months after our breakup, he told me about Isabel, Robin, and Coby. He first met Isabel a couple of years ago, when they both participated in a project to restore a stone reef off the coast. Now, they had crossed paths again, and it turned out that Isabel and her wife Robin were looking for someone to have children with. So far, they had an arrangement with their friend Coby, who was nonbinary, but they would like to include a fourth person. Natan liked all three of them, and they liked him too. It seemed to be exactly what he was looking for.

I found myself being somewhat puzzled. Now that I was no longer part of the equation, why didn't he just find another girlfriend who wanted children? And for that matter, why didn't Isabel and Robin just use a sperm bank? But probably, this was just outdated thinking on my part. You could have lots of reasons for deliberately choosing an alternative to the two-parent nuclear family.

They started looking for a place to live. Natan showed me pictures of the houses they were considering, and a while later, I was introduced to the three people who comprised his new family. Meeting them was a curious mix of entirely unproblematic and really tough. Unproblematic because Natan had explained the whole situation to them, so none of us had to conceal anything. But for the same reason, my difficult emotions surfaced. Natan and I had loved each other. Now the four of them were planning something that comprised the very reason we had separated.

I had to remind myself that it wasn't Isabel, Robin, and Coby who took him away from me. It had been my own choice as well as his, not theirs. Natan was no longer my partner, but a friend who was about to attain the life he wanted to live. If I felt a certain jealousy towards the people, he would share it with, I had better keep it to myself.

Then they found their home. The house was spacious, complete with a large garden and several outbuildings; plenty of room for both adults and children, not to mention projects and hobbies. Now, Natan would be able to pursue all his various interests in his own home. As he showed me around, speaking about his plans for renovations, growing ventures and biological experiments, I honestly felt a joyful anticipation on his behalf. I now realized how much he had shaped his life around my needs and wishes, not only with regards to children, but also in the way we had lived, in small apartments, with a tiny balcony at the most, providing space for a few plant boxes.

This realization made our breakup easier to bear. It confirmed we had made the right decision; that the love we shared wasn't enough to fill our lives. Anyway, our love wasn't lost. We still cared for each other, and although it could be hurtful to see him, my emotions had begun to fall into place.

I followed their endeavors setting up the house. Then I was informed that Isabel was pregnant. I visited a few times during her pregnancy, and once again when the child was born; a little boy whom they named Dale. Natan's child, I thought as I held him for the first time. Their common child, who could have been mine as well. A pang of sorrow snuck into my happiness for them. Not because I was excluded from this family, but because I didn't wish to be part of it.

If any lingering doubt remained, it vanished when the familiar radio signals announced the arrival of another zoi. I had long ago applied for participation in the next expedition, this time as one of the experienced crew members. Kiah had done the same, and we were both selected. Sipho joined as the only veteran of two previous expeditions, while the rest of the crew consisted of newcomers. One of them we knew in advance, Dr. Evardo Mendoza. It turned out that he had been training for years, developing the necessary skills, and his medical expertise would no doubt be highly useful.

The journey we had so long prepared for would now become a reality. Natan had his child, and I was about to get what I so ardently wished for. My first encounter with the zois would not be the only one. I would have a second chance of getting close to the being that had become the center of my existence. My life revolved around space and the zois. Everything else was secondary.

HABITAT

When I return to the living room, Amira is on her way in from the passageway leading to our quarters. A jolt runs through me, and I clutch the entrance frame, keeping myself in the opening. She does the same, giving me an oddly frightened look. Not angry, which I would have understood. For so long we have been inseparably linked, and now I have left without any explanation. Is it a guilty conscience that now makes my heart pound at the mere sight of her? That's usually how I react when I get too close to others, but a few minutes ago, I got very close to Linn and Evardo, even touched them, without my body protesting. Now it's my twin I don't feel like approaching.

We hover in our respective openings. Once again, I count the entrance holes. There's still one too many. Where does it lead?

"Which one of them is it?"

She sounds as if she's talking to herself, but I reply anyway.

"Maybe we can figure it out. I'm on my way from Linn's quarters. Are you coming from ours?"

The word *ours* takes a strange shape in my mouth. The intimacy that it entails now seems so claustrophobic. Apparently to her as well, judging from the face she makes.

"I am. Which means that on this side, we have the usual number." She nods in the direction which to me is right, and to her is left. "It has to be one of the others."

There are four holes to the left of me. Two of them will lead to Evardo's and Kiah's quarters, a third to the pantry, and the fourth to some unknown place. Usually, the distribution of the openings relating to the oblong shape of the room tells us which one leads where, but the holes in themselves are essentially identical, and the new one doesn't stand out from the others in any noticeable way.

"So... should we just pick one each?" I ask without moving. She, too, seems frozen, unable to leave her opening.

"You go first." A slight chuckle in her voice addresses the absurdity of the situation. We're like two children standing on the diving board at the swimming pool, equally afraid to make the jump. What exactly are we afraid of? I take a few, deep breaths. My fear retreats, replaced by excitement. A new entrance appearing just now is hardly a coincidence. It may contain the key to understanding everything that has happened recently.

"Okay." I tighten my grip on the entrance frame and pull myself in a curve towards the nearest opening.

It's a connecting passage like all the others, just unusually long. When I reach the opening at the other end, I stop and look around, confused. This is the very same room I just left. The living room. Same oblong shape, same number of entrances. Have I been led in a circle?

Again, I count the entrance holes. One on each end of the room, three in the opposite side, and—I move out into the room to be able to see them all—four in the room behind me, including the one I came through. Still one too many, but only one. If the passageway simply led back to the living room, there ought to be two. This isn't the living room. It's a copy of it.

The zoi has grown, that's what Evardo said right after the separation. It has been stretching, not only to accommodate more organelles, but also more air pockets; more places for us to live. New rooms have been added to the habitat before, but we have never seen an existing room being copied.

I look around at the holes in the walls. How far does the duplication extend? I'd better go see for myself.

It's not just the living room. A quick survey of the adjacent rooms shows that they are all there: the lavatory, the pantry, the holoroom. I conclude that the entrances to each of Linn's, Evardo's, and Kiah's bedchambers are in the right place, and then proceed to my own quarters. As I open the entrance, I feel almost convinced that Amira will be inside. But the room is empty, at least of people.

Two sleeping bags are floating in mid-air. A few small objects are keeping them company, having snuck out of the grid in the furthermost end, just as usual. I propel myself over there, open the grid and start looking through the items in it. First, clothes and utility items, then my personal keepsakes. Every crew member was allowed to bring two kilos worth of items without any practical use. Quite a lot for a space flight, but this expedition differed from all others by being of a permanent nature. ETLEA's psychologists deemed it necessary for us to bring something to remind us of the life we had left behind forever.

Most of my keepsakes are decorative items given

to me by various people. To keep them in place, I have gathered them in a few bags. Many have a separate casing, and when I try opening one of them, it's empty. It should have contained a necklace that was a present from Natan. One by one, I open the rest of the casings. Some are empty, but not all. A few other pieces of jewelry are missing, and so is a replica of one of the peculiar bronze figurines from Luristan. But my collection of little animal figures meticulously carved in wood and bone, brought home from various corners of the world by Karim, reside within their boxes. A ram is missing its eyes, though. They were made of glass.

Of course. The common denominator for the missing items is that they were made from non-organic material: glass, stone, or metal. The zoi hasn't been able to generate them, as it can apparently do with any biological substance, including the synthetic plastic materials used for the vast majority of our utility items.

Hastily, I pack it all away and return to the holoroom. The projector is in its case, and when I press On, it starts up. I turn it off again. A proper test of its functionality is more than I'm up for right now. My hands tremble, and I can barely operate the buttons. The projector is pure BB-tech, or at least I think so. It might contain some metallic or mineral components. Linn would know.

Linn. I haven't looked inside her bedchamber yet.

Will the version of her who is almost assimilated into the zoi be stuck in the wall as a feature of the room? I have to check.

Moving through the passageways, I try to calm my trembling body. Why do I react so strongly? I'm not even sure what emotion my agitated state represents—fear or excitement or something in between. My head is buzzing with thoughts I can't fully process. My restlessness compels me to stay in motion, roaming this new habitat, not only to answer the question about what it contains or lacks, but simply to sense the place. Take it in.

With frantic movements, I open the entrance to Linn's bedchamber. There's no Linn-shaped relief in the wall, but I see some changes in the structure of the wall, precisely where the two Linns have their nest in the original room. The surface is uneven, with bumps and bulges, slightly undulating. Horrified by the sight, I still continue towards it, reaching out to touch the soft, yielding membrane. It draws me to it, gently, while tongues and threads grow from the membrane, enveloping my hand.

I pull it back in a jerk. The tongues release their grip, wavering in the air for a few seconds as if they are searching for something to latch on to, and then retreat into the wall. I stare at them as they vanish, once again incapable of characterizing my emotions by any specific term. There's an element of disgust, of a primal fear of being eaten, but at the same time, I'm fascinated, even infatuated. Part of me wants to touch the wall once more, to let it enclose me. Is it the zoi influencing me? Is it luring me in, intending to swallow me up, like it seems to be doing with both versions of Linn?

"Amira?"

It's Kiah's voice. She calls once more, and I disentangle myself, following the sound through the passageway back into the living room. She floats in there, together with an Evardo. One of each.

Kiah's eyes widen at the sight of me. Evardo rushes toward me.

"What happened?" he asks. "Are you hurt?"

I shake my head silently, glancing down at myself, half expecting to find wounds or blood or something that would explain their reaction. But my naked body is unharmed. It must be the expression on my face that's making them uneasy, and perhaps the fact that I'm still trembling.

"I'm fine," I manage to say. They regard me skeptically, and I continue, "I'm just overwhelmed. All of this..." I nod towards the openings in the living room wall, "It seems to be an exact replica of the rooms we live in. And not just the rooms, but every object in them. Except for the few made of non-organic materials."

"An exact replica," Evardo repeats. "But with no humans in it, except for us?"

"Exactly. No humans. Not even Linn."

Kiah sends us both a puzzled look. Apparently, she doesn't know about the situation with Linn. I assume she has hardly given her a thought since she got her own twin. On the other hand, how much have I done for Linn? While the shadows emerged, she and I were practically an item, and then I left her to fend for herself. Evardo has been the only one making an effort to help her.

"They are both stuck in their bedchamber wall," he explains. "The zoi sustains them, which is the only reason they're still alive. But it has consequences, especially for one of them. I have never seen her conscious. Ever since the separation, she has been shrinking and growing deeper into the membrane."

"She seems more like a part of the room than a person," I add. "But evidently, the zoi still regards her as an independent being, since she hasn't been part of this replication. At the same time..." I pause for a moment to get a grip on myself. "It looks like the wall is ready for her. A soft area that draws you in. I've just touched it. It was... pretty scary."

Evardo gives me an inquiring look. "So that's why you're in shock."

Am I in shock? Perhaps I am, but not to an extent that keeps me from reasoning. My inner swarm of chaotic thoughts starts to take shape. Duplication, this time not of us, but our habitat. Linn's room, waiting for her. The zoi replicating everything it contains, while also growing and expanding. It all points in the same direction. Why haven't I seen it before?

The zoi is about to divide itself.

CONVERSATION

It felt like a reunion, and in a sense, that's exactly what it was, even if the zoi who now welcomed us wasn't the same we had visited during the previous expedition. This entity hadn't yet encountered a human being, and all processes had to start from scratch: the formation of airlocks prompted by our proximity, the first physical contact, and the resulting creation of air pockets. But it all followed the same patterns as last time. The first biological samples of zoi material confirmed that this was yet another clone of the specimens we had encountered before. Genetically speaking, they were the same being.

We, too, reacted like we had done before, with nausea and unease during an adaptation phase of varying length. Personally, I surpassed the discomfort a little faster this time, perhaps because my organism was prepared for it, perhaps simply because I knew it would pass.

Most of us remained in the zoi throughout the expedition. Only Sipho and one of the newcomers, an astrophysicist named Marina, alternated between staying in the zoi and the space shuttle. This meant they had to go through a new adaptation phase each time they had been absent for longer periods of time. Evardo meticulously monitored these repeated reactions along with the steadier progression among the rest of us. He was somewhat worried about another newcomer, the young BB-tech expert, Linn, whose hormone levels kept fluctuating. But Linn claimed this didn't affect her, and with all her hard work on the experimentation with zoi substances we had to assume it was true.

My own task was studying the biology of our host, with a primary focus on the various organelles; attempting to determine their respective functions and describe the interplay between them. I only had time to scratch the surface, working in a frenzy while the weeks turned into months.

One day Kiah came by, interrupting my work.

"Set that aside for a moment," she said with a gesture towards the screen I was hovering by. "I have a problem I'd like to discuss with you."

"Can't you ask Sipho?" I replied, not taking my eyes off my notes. "I'm a little busy right now."

"I want to discuss it with *you*. You're always busy. I would be too if I were getting anywhere with my own assignments, but that's exactly the problem. I'm stuck."

It dawned on me that Kiah had seemed restless lately, perhaps for quite a while. I had noticed it without giving it a second thought, without asking her what the matter was.

"But weren't you always aware that it's an impossible task?" Now I looked at her. Knowing Kiah, I clearly sensed her frustration, perhaps even anger. "You're attempting to communicate with a creature that most likely doesn't think at all. To understand its psychology, though it doesn't seem to be sentient. No one can blame you for struggling to come up with any concrete results."

"Struggling to, yes, that's perfectly fine. But we've been here for over four months, and I have achieved absolutely nothing! In total, we have less than a year, then it's back to Earth. Back to developing elaborate theories I have no way of testing. Back to waiting for another zoi to maybe show up, and then hope I'll be chosen once more for the next expedition. But why would I be if I'm not making any progress?"

"Don't you think ETLEA will recognize that these things take time? They know you. They will understand that you're doing your best."

She gave a despairing sigh. "Exactly. I'm doing my very best, and it's not enough. At least, it hasn't been so far. And no, I'm not giving up, but I need to talk this over with someone who understands what

I'm talking about. If you can tear yourself away for just a moment, I'll be very obliged."

"Of course." I felt guilty for being such a lousy friend. But rectifying my behavior was better that self-reproach. "Tell me about your efforts and why they haven't worked out."

So she did, describing a wide array of systematic observations combined with ingenious attempts at interaction. All they had achieved was confirming what we already knew: the zoi's organism constituted a highly complex system. Interaction between its various elements seemed to be at least partly governed by chemical signals, but understanding the workings of these signals in any meaningful detail remained far beyond our reach. For that very reason, trying our own hand at them was much too risky. We would have very little clue what we were signaling, which would make the zoi's reaction dangerously unpredictable.

"Then we'll just have to keep observing and recording," I interjected. "Isn't that good enough?"

"It is for you. That's your method as a biologist, and you could easily do the necessary registering without me." Kiah crossed her arms. "Later on, psychologists back on Earth could try to infer a pattern, and in several decades, we may be able to send some kind of intelligible signal to the zois, provided they keep appearing. For my effort to make any sense, I need to identify a pattern right now, and then send some kind of signal—one that I know the meaning of myself—and get a response I can understand, or at least interpret. Otherwise, ETLEA will simply consider it a waste of valuable space to have a psychologist as part of the crew."

A response I can understand. Those words reminded me of something, a half-forgotten idea formed a long time ago, even before I became an astronaut. A notion that might be naive, but Kiah was desperately searching for a way forward. Even a silly idea was better than nothing.

"Couldn't you say that in some sense we're already communicating?" I hesitantly asked. "We're addressing the zoi simply by being here, by exhibiting signs of various physical needs, and it replies by fulfilling them. I mean, it's pretty trivial, but looking at it from that perspective could perhaps be helpful."

Kiah's face had frozen. She was staring into the air, in my direction, but without seeing me.

"You're right," she said. "You're totally damn fucking obviously right! We're speaking to the zoi by just being present. We could do a lot more than that, not by mimicking its chemical signals, but by utilizing our own biology, actively and deliberately."

"So, you know how to do that?" I asked, but Kiah was already on her way out.

"Not entirely. But probably... if I think it over, all by myself... thank you Amira!" Briefly, she turned towards me, sending me a radiant smile. "This was exactly what I needed."

A week passed, then Kiah arrived at one of our meetings with a plan.

"I intend to present the zoi with a stool sample."

"A stool sample?" Yuze repeated, sounding incredulous. He was one of the newcomers, a geneticist focusing on mapping the differences and similarities between the zoi's genetic material and our own. He and Kiah didn't get along too well.

"Yes, such a sample will provide the zoi with a new basis for understanding our biology. Probably it already snatched a bit of feces and urine from the toilets, but it could still make a difference if it receives a larger quantity."

Linn made a face. "A difference for what?" she asked.

"We'll see." Kiah smiled broadly. "This is a way of providing the zoi with information about us, like we already do through our skin and our breath. Only now we're doing it on purpose."

"To me it sounds like an unnecessary risk," Yuze said. "What if the zoi reacts in some undesirable way?"

"It won't," Kiah stated. "We're not acting blindly here. We're adding a line to an ongoing conversation in which the zoi has consistently answered by giving us what we need."

"I don't know." Marina looked around at the others. "It seems a bit... impolite, doesn't it?"

Kiah gave an impatient sigh. "If anything, it's impolite not to do it! Think about what would normally happen when the zoi assimilates another life form. This life form would naturally submit all waste products to its host, while we're withholding some of ours because we perceive them as unclean. But that isn't a universal fact. Lots of animal species interact with their own feces quite closely. Some of them even eat it."

More grimacing. Linn looked as if she had to keep herself from vomiting.

"I'm sorry," Kiah said, lifting a hand. "I'm just trying to make the case for this being the logical next step. And I'll deposit the sample out in the cytosol, not too close to the habitat."

Evardo nodded thoughtfully. "The zoi is affecting us as it is. Giving it a better foundation for doing so will probably be to our advantage."

"Precisely! And because we're provoking a response, we have a better chance of studying the process. When and how does the zoi react? Will we be able to continue the interaction we're initiating? We'll speak to it using the language of biology and examine the response from both angles: natural science and communications theory."

"As long as we're not forgetting the health aspect," Evardo added. "But I'll see to that part."

TELOS

'm waiting in the living room while Kiah and Evardo explore the new habitat. Neither of them seems particularly surprised about its existence. They probably long since figured out what is going on.

I'm still struggling with the idea, though its logic now appears self-evident. On its way in through the solar system, the zoi has been gathering raw materials in the form of asteroids containing all the elements it needs. During its orbit around the sun, it has been absorbing vast amounts of energy. Using that combination of energy and corporeal matter, it is now in the process of doubling all it contains in order to split itself in two, like cells do. What we are currently experiencing corresponds to the telophase, the final stage of cell division or mitosis, in which everything has been copied and the cell is getting ready for the split. Telos means conclusion. It concludes the mitosis, but also the life of the old cell. Once the division is completed, this cell no longer exists. It has been replaced by two newly created ones.

All of this is entirely in line with my own theories. It looks as if I didn't really take them seriously, or maybe I just couldn't imagine them having such concrete consequences for myself. I have been integrated into the zoi's organism as a new addition to it. This will obviously include me in its reproduction.

I made the choice of embarking on this journey. Whatever happens now is a consequence of that choice. Those consequences have affected the four of us differently: Linn is succumbing to them. Kiah embraces them, thriving in the constant changes. Evardo handles them calmly and rationally, focusing on how to be of help to the rest of us. And me? I'm fighting back, refusing to accept things as they are, though time and again I find myself defeated by the circumstances.

Kiah and Evardo return.

"We have almost everything here," Evardo says. "I'm only missing a few metallic instruments. Maybe I can ask the other Evardo to let me have some of his."

"Why?" Kiah gazes into the air with the distant stare that I find so frightening. "We will have to learn how to manage without that kind of thing. Let the others keep them if they want."

"So you will just stay here?" I ask. "Without going

to get anything? Without saying goodbye?"

She shrugs. "I have no need to say goodbye. We have become separate units. Drawing out the breach will only make things harder."

The worst part is, she's probably right. The mere thought of a farewell seems unbearable, and besides, my body protests against re-entering the old habitat. It belongs here, with one Kiah and one Evardo, and it's strongly averse to being confronted with any double, theirs as well as its own. That would violate the logic of the telophase, contradict the impulses currently forcing everything in the zoi to seek out opposite ends, away from corresponding components, from everything belonging to the other of the two cells undergoing the process of separating from each other. But my body's reactions shouldn't dictate my choices. Besides, there's one questions we still need to address.

"What about Linn?"

Kiah turns to Evardo. "Yes, what about Linn? Her bedchamber is ready to receive her, but you're telling me that both versions of her are joined into the wall of the old habitat. Will it even be possible for her to move from there?"

"I would consider it possible," Evardo replies. "But such a transferal will be extremely strenuous for her, and she's already weak. Each moment she's detached will shorten the time she has left, and that isn't long to begin with."

A wave of sorrow washes over me. I'm going to

lose Linn, I already know that; there's nothing I can do to prevent it. But to some extent, I can choose the manner in which I lose her.

"I'm going back to her," I state. "With or without you."

"To say goodbye?" Kiah looks as if her mind is elsewhere. Does Linn really mean so little to her?

"To ask if there's anything I can do for her. But yes, also to say goodbye, to her and to all of them. Because that's what you do. What humans do." My carotid arteries are throbbing. I can't keep the anger out of my voice. "You may be ready to forget who you are—to follow all impulses from the zoi like an obedient organelle. I intend to hold on to my own will and to my humanity. That's why I'm going back through that passage, even though it will be unpleasant."

Kiah gives no reply, but gazes towards the opening of the connecting passageway, still with a preoccupied expression on her face. Meanwhile, Evardo nods.

"I'll come with you, Amira."

"So will I." Kiah's voice does not reveal any kind of emotion. This total lack of reaction it makes me even angrier, but this isn't the right time to start a row.

"Well, let's go, then," I say, pushing off towards the passage.

The old version of the living room is empty, but the sound of voices filters out from the corridor leading to Linn's bedchamber. Every fiber of my being is resisting. Back in the new habitat, the situation was in some sense normal: one of me, one of Kiah and Evardo respectively. My reluctance to re-encounter the doubles isn't exclusively caused by zoi-induced impulses, but also by a profoundly human fear of the incomprehensible. In a factual sense, I more or less know what is happening, but I still can't grasp it. How could I, an individual being possessing my own personality, intellect, and complex emotional life, become a component in something as primitive and impersonal as cell division?

I take a deep breath, then plunge into the opening with Evardo and Kiah following me. Ahead of us, I hear the other versions of them conversing. Among the voices is also the one that's so close to being my own. The voice of the other Amira.

All three of them float outside Linn's quarters. I stop some distance away, and we hang there facing each other, in two separate groups. I sense Kiah and Evardo next to me, but deliberately avoid looking at them. Instead, I watch the other set of people in front of me, observing their reactions. Evardo stiffens, but slowly regains his composed expression. Kiah looks surprised at first, then nods and smiles. Amira's initial shock at seeing us is replaced by a wariness that seems almost hostile. My own heart is hammering in my chest. I have no desire to approach her, but does she really have to glare like that?

"We have come to say goodbye." My voice sounds hollow and weak. The words seem empty and trivial. Was it a mistake to return? The three individuals in front of me feel like strangers. It was probably entirely random who ended up with whom, but now we have formed our separate units. Us and them.

The other Kiah raises her eyebrows. "Is that all?" she asks.

Next to me, Evardo clears is throat. "First and foremost, we have come for Linn's sake. Because both versions of her are here."

"And now you will take her away!" This comes from Amira as a bitter outburst. I open my mouth to contradict her, to emphasize that we have only come for a farewell. Why would we bring Linn with us, only to have her die in our hands? But Kiah beats me to the reply.

"Only if she wants to," she says. "If she prefers to stay here, with her twin and the three of you, we'll leave it at that."

Everybody, including Amira, seems to understand something that eludes me. They ask no questions; don't seem to wonder why we have this discussion.

"I'll make it very clear to her what the risks are," Evardo adds. "Being relocated to the new habitat will severely weaken her. I can't guarantee she'll survive it."

"Then why would we do it?" I ask.

No one answers my question. After a while, the other Evardo speaks:

"As you say, it should be her own choice. Now, go talk to her. Then we'll see."

He pulls away from the entrance. Amira lingers in front of it, but the other Kiah places a hand on her arm. The familiarity of that touch is almost as painful to me as Amira's hostility. Something has happened between the two of them that hasn't happened between me and my Kiah. Tears well up in Amira's eyes, but her grim expression softens, and she follows along. Kiah whispers something that I can't hear. A shiver runs through Amira, and when they stop farther down the passageway, she turns to look at me once again.

The accusation is gone from her gaze, but it's still filled with sorrow. In that moment, I wish we still belonged together. That we were still forced to overcome every disagreement, untangle every misunderstanding, because we couldn't bear to be separate. But the forces which used to keep us together are now pushing us apart.

My Evardo and Kiah have already passed through the entrance to Linn's bedchamber. It's for her sake that I'm here, I remind myself. Regardless of how this will end, I must talk to her. Either to see her for the last time, or to take her with me. Though right now, I don't understand why I would.

SUSTENANCE

Kiah immediately set her plan into motion. Wearing her spacesuit and oxygen supply, she ventured out into the liquid-filled environment that we seldom visited at this point, placing her stool sample in it.

At first, nothing much seemed to happen, except for the sample slowly dissolving and seemingly disappearing. The zoi had absorbed it, and now we could only wait and see if it would have any kind of effect.

A day passed, and then we discovered a new kind of outgrowth in one of the smaller air pockets, located at the opposite end of the habitat. When we analyzed them, they turned out to be a sort of concentrated nutrition, complete with vitamins, minerals, fibers, and a perfectly balanced combination of proteins, carbohydrates, and different types of fats. The analysis revealed no traces of anything potentially harmful, but Evardo still warned against attempting to consume the substance.

"It would be wiser to first bring some of it back to Earth for a more careful examination," he said, taking hold of the container with the collected nutrition.

"Wiser?" Kiah looked at him in disbelief. "It would be completely idiotic! Finally, we have something like a conversation going on—one in which we are an active part. We sent the zoi a message, and it has responded. Now you want to stop at that, just because of an entirely hypothetical risk to our health?"

"I see no reason to take such a risk," Evardo replied. "We are already bringing home plenty of results, including the effects our very presence in the zoi has on our bodies."

"*You* may have plenty of results, but *I* haven't." Kiah reached out her hand towards him. "Give me some of it, please."

Evardo hesitated for a few seconds. Probably realizing he wouldn't be able to deter her, he opened the lid, took out a small lump, and handed it to Kiah. She put it in her mouth, chewed a couple of times, and wrinkled her nose. Then she swallowed the lump.

"Not much of a culinary experience," she remarked. "But not directly repulsive either."

We all stared at her, waiting for signs of poisoning, allergic reaction, any kind of physical response. But minutes passed, and nothing happened.

"Well," she finally said to Evardo "Does this reassure you?"

"Only temporarily," he replied. "I would like to keep you under observation for at least a day."

Kiah rolled her eyes but didn't protest.

"In the meantime, no one will eat any more of it," Evardo continued with a stern gaze, first at Kiah, then at the rest of us.

I had considered following Kiah's example. Leaving her to take this risk alone felt a bit cowardly. But of course, the rational strategy would be starting out with one person and only expanding the experiment after carefully monitoring her reactions. Besides, I wasn't sure if Kiah wanted me to interfere. This was her idea, a potential breakthrough in the area where she had been stuck for so long. I wouldn't take that away from her.

Next day, Kiah was still feeling fine. She ate another lump, a larger one this time, and then let the zoi have another stool sample, placed in the same location as the last one. A new air bubble was beginning to grow next to this spot, she told me when she returned.

"What is it trying to say?" she asked, furrowing her brow, then answered her own question: "I suppose it's attempting to make it easier for us to dispose of the waste matter. Once the new bubble is connected to the rest of the habitat, we could use it as a toilet, replacing the one we brought with us."

"And how does the zoi expect that to work in practice?" I couldn't help sounding skeptical. "Should we just go in there and relieve ourselves in mid-air?"

It was meant as a rhetorical question, but Kiah seemed to consider the matter. "Either that or into the membrane," she replied. Then she noticed my disgusted expression. "Okay, that sounds pretty gross. But how about if we move the toilet equipment over there and connect it to the wall? Instead of pumping our excrements into a tank, it could deliver it to the zoi, without leaving it to float around. And besides—" she brightened, "—besides, this is a statement in itself. We're making use of the possibilities it offers but combining them with our own solutions."

"Do you think the zoi will get that message?" I asked.

"I hope so. We're demonstrating that our technology can connect with its own organic system. If we're lucky, it will start treating tech equipment as integrable. At least the biologically based technology."

Something in her tone made me uneasy.

"And if we're not lucky?"

"Then we might be calling attention to technology as a disruptive element," Kiah said with a shrug. "In earlier cases, the zois have destroyed all devices left within them, once the humans were gone. I suspect that the same could happen as soon as the zoi has a firm grasp on how to keep us alive. It may still need to establish a clear division between life form and equipment of a biological nature, but sooner or later, it will have made that division, and it will start cleaning up what it perceives as superfluous."

"Then this experiment is much too dangerous! If you really believe it could go that way, we shouldn't take the risk."

"We need to do it." Kiah looked around and continued in a hushed voice. "This way, we may be may be able to influence the process that is already happening, show the zoi that technological objects are important to us, even when they aren't strictly necessary for our survival."

I could see the logic, but still, it was scary that our actions could have that kind of consequence.

"How can you be so calm about it? You're negotiating with the zoi's response pattern without really having a clue how it works. One poorly chosen message on our part, and suddenly we're left with no equipment at all."

Kiah regarded me with her head askew.

"Amira, what exactly do you think we're doing here? Of course, something like that might happen, or far worse than that. We're exposing ourselves to immense danger just by being here inside the zoi. Sometimes, I get the impression that this doesn't really register with you. That you think it's all a game."

A game. I caught myself laughing at her words,

because there was some truth to them. My childhood conception of the zois still governed how I perceived them. Behind my scientific approach lay an unwavering belief in their good intentions. Like some misunderstood yet peaceful beast from the animated holo-movies I loved as a child, they would harbor a benevolent consciousness beneath the unfathomable surface. Kiah couldn't take refuge in such naive notions, precisely because she had been tasked with understanding the zois like they truly were, from a psychology that was at best a metaphor.

"And I thought you and I were so alike!" I exclaimed. "But you're right: when it comes to the zois, I'm probably a bit naive. All we have to judge them by are a few brief visits, and we have no idea what would happen to someone who took up permanent residence in one of them."

"Exactly!" A fire ignited in Kiah's gaze. "We have no idea. But we may find out."

"What do you mean?" I asked, even though I had a pretty good idea what she would say. I had been thinking along the same lines ever since we realized that the zoi had started producing nourishment for us.

"What I mean is that we'll soon be able to stay for good. To remain in a zoi when it leaves the solar system. If it's able to supply us with sustenance, just like it supplies us with oxygen; if it can take care of our waste products by incorporating them into its internal biological cycle, then nothing really prevents us from doing so."

"No, but—you don't mean right now, do you? You're not planning to stay in this zoi?"

Kiah ran her fingertips over the nearby wall membrane. "Not this one. But next time, when we understand the workings of the zoi a little better. That's precisely why we need to advance this understanding as much as possible, within your field as well as mine and everyone else's. But especially mine."

"Why are you in such a hurry? Isn't it better to give it some time? Become truly familiar with the zois through expeditions like this. And then, in a few decades—"

"In a few decades, there may not be any more zois arriving," Kiah interrupted. "And even if they keep coming, in thirty- or forty-years' time it won't be us, you and me, who get the chance to inhabit one of them. With luck we will be chosen for one more expedition, maybe even two. But that will be it."

Those were thoughts I had dismissed myself. The important thing was exploring the zois, not my personal role in this exploration. I couldn't expect to occupy a spot on every future expedition. Others would take my place, achieve new results, a higher degree of connection and insight. That's how these things went, how they needed to go. Besides, I had to want more of life than this. Didn't I?

"If we leave, we will never return," I muttered. "The zoi will travel into interstellar space, and we can do nothing but follow along."

"Probably. But even that would be something no human being has yet experienced. Traveling into space, not just a quick jaunt to the Moon or Mars, but away from the solar system and further out, in a vessel that won't need to carry any supplies of oxygen, water, or food. And who knows: With time we may learn to truly communicate with the zoi we're inhabiting. Maybe we'll be able to steer its course. Possibilities may unfold that we can't even imagine."

"Or we may live out the remaining decades of our brief human lives within an enclosed space, in the midst of absolute nothingness, centuries away from reaching the next star, until we die of old age or boredom."

Kiah shook her head. "Not boredom. There will be so much to investigate and discover. Just having the chance to observe the zoi in another part of its life cycle would be incredible."

"And risky."

"Yes, of course! But will we let that stop us, or do we view the risk as part of the adventure? We don't know what will happen. That's precisely what makes it exciting."

TRANSPLANTING

It's only been a few hours since my last visit to Linn's chamber, but in the meantime, everything has changed. I wondered how much time I would have to spend with a dying Linn. Now the question is whether the dying Linn is coming with me, or if it's here and now we say goodbye forever.

They're both asleep when we enter, the large and the small version of her. We wait in silence. I don't want to be the one to wake her, even though my own body is flooded with stress hormones telling me I need to get away from here, back to where I belong. It's not just me. Evardo's breathing sounds strained. Kiah is surrounded by a haze of sweat droplets. The wait feels like an eternity, but it's probably just a few minutes before the larger Linn awakes.

It takes her a moment to focus. When she finally speaks, her voice is weak, yet sounds surprisingly steady.

"You are the others, aren't you?"

"Yes," Kiah replies. "We make up the group that has found a home elsewhere, in a habitat identical to this one. Your chamber is part of it. The wall is ready to receive you."

"So, you have come to collect me?" Now Linn's voice is quivering a bit.

"Only if you want us to," Kiah replies. "But I hope you do. We won't pressure you, but—"

"Exactly. We won't," Evardo cuts her off. "It's Linn's own choice, regardless of what any of us might wish for." He turns to Linn. "If you prefer to stay here, I completely understand. The transfer will be tough on you, perhaps even fatal. Besides, I suspect you don't feel the same urge as the rest of us, to distance yourself from your twin. Perhaps you even need to stay together?"

"I... don't know." Linn looks at the little being beside her. "Sometimes it feels like we are melding again, becoming one with the zoi and each other. But then these waves of panic hit me, and I want to get away."

Her gaze locks onto mine. I recognize the longing within it, an instinct as powerful as my own. Then her expression softens, and she reaches out towards the little Linn, touching what barely resembles a hand, more like a root extending into the membrane. In a sense, that's what it is. She has roots deep within the zoi, as a tree in the soil. The small Linn has firmly established herself by now. Transplanting her to a new environment is out of the question. But the bigger Linn is like a cutting, with roots that might still be loosened and find new ground.

"It makes me feel so cruel. That I want to leave her."

"But is that truly cruel?" Kiah asks, ignoring a warning glance from Evardo. "She will have the zoi, along with the other versions of us. And they have her, while we lack you."

"Lack me?" Linn bitterly chuckles. "I wouldn't be of much use. It's all a matter of time before I won't be here at all. Not as myself, but merely as a part of the zoi."

"Exactly. As part of the zoi." The pupils in Kiah's eyes dilate, and she emphasizes the following words: "You will be present! In the zoi, along with us, as a part of the entity we all belong to. Now and in the future."

Her words send shivers down my spine. The very notion of such an entity, one in which I'm merely a component, terrifies me to the core. At the same time, I feel a tiny twinkle of curiosity, a desire to experience the unity Kiah speaks of. Is that just another reaction induced by chemical signals from the zoi? I can't be certain, but it feels like a genuine emotion. One originating within myself.

Evardo takes Linn's hand. "If you stay here, we will miss you terribly. But we'll manage. If you choose to accompany us, you should make that choice for your own sake, not ours."

Linn smiles at him, giving his hand a squeeze, then looks at me questioningly.

"And you, Amira? You're not saying anything?"

What am I supposed to say? I'm busy enough keeping up with the conversation as well as my shifting emotions. Linn reaches for me, and before I know it, we're holding each other, as tightly as we can without her leaving the membrane.

"I'm so sorry," I whisper. "I should have tried harder to help you."

"But that's not what we're talking about right now. We're discussing what happens next, not just to me, but to all of us." Linn frees herself from my embrace. There's an assessing quality both in her tone and her gaze. "Do you want me to come?"

What holds me back from answering isn't just Evardo's admonitions. If Linn comes along, I will have to watch her shrink and merge with the zoi. Maybe it's better to lose her now, while preserving the memory of the person she was.

"I need you to answer," she firmly states. "Not what you think I want to hear. Not what you believe is best for me. But how you truly feel."

I don't know what I truly feel. I don't know what I

want. Maybe I just want to give up. I catch myself yearning for the tranquility expressed by the sleeping features of the little Linn. Then a movement from Kiah captures my attention, and once again, the twinkle of curiosity stirs within me. I'll never be as fearless as her, eagerly embracing every change and upheaval we're exposed to. But I may be able to face those changes with acceptance. I could try to find my own path within them, alongside Kiah and Evardo—and in a way, also Linn.

"Yes, I want you to come," I say. "But I don't want to harm you; I'd rather leave you here."

Linn takes a trembling breath. "I know it will be tough. But with your help, I'll make it. Perhaps..." She hesitates a moment before continuing. "Will you hold me, Amira? While you're transporting me, I mean. With your body against my back, I won't feel as fragile."

Blood drains from my face. She's asking me to take the place of the wall membrane, to connect my skin with hers, touching the areas of her body through which the zoi is currently taking it over. Could she infect me with her dependency on it? But I have failed her too often already. If this will help her, I have to do it.

"Of course," I reply is calmly as I can. "Do you need to prepare for it?"

She shakes her head. "Let's get it over with."

Kiah and Evardo approach from their respective sides.

"We have every reason to hurry," Kiah says. "The passage between the two habitats might close any moment now."

She wraps her arm around Linn to lift her from the membrane but withdraws when Evardo raises a hand to stop her.

"Are you sure about this?" he asks Linn.

"Yes. Yes, I am. I want to go with you." She grabs hold of my hand, firmly, as if she's about to pull herself free. Then she loosens her grip and turns towards her twin, reaching out to caress her cheek. "Goodbye, sister. I wish you well, you and the zoi that you will be part of."

The little being stays completely still. I'm not sure if I'm imagining the slight twitch at the corners of her mouth, suggesting something as human as a smile. She too was once my friend, and this is our final goodbye. I let the impression of that faint smile settle within my memory, hoping that it carries some kind of message. That in her strange and uncanny condition, she has found a sort of happiness, and that she wishes us well on our journey.

The others are still waiting in the passageway; the Evardo, Kiah and Amira who aren't us, the twins we are now forced to leave behind for good. They move aside when the four of us emerge from the bedchamber, with Kiah in the lead and Evardo behind Linn and me, nudging us forward while Kiah helps us along from the other side. Linn's back and bottom press against my chest and hips. She used to be taller than me, but now she feels like a child. Her skin is sticky with some kind of zoi substance, but my initial disgust is already waning. There's no time to think of anything but moving Linn to her chamber in the new habitat, as quickly and painlessly as possible.

"So, you will be taking her with you," the other Evardo observes.

"She made her own decision," his reflection, my Evardo, replies. "And now we need to act in a hurry. There's no time for a long farewell."

"But hopefully for a brief one." That comes from the other Kiah as she floats towards us. My Kiah makes way for her, and I realize she's about to touch us. Yet, my body fails to react with the expected revulsion, perhaps because the breach is now a reality. We're on our way out of here, back to our own place. That allows room for one last touch.

It takes the shape of a kiss, Kiah's lips against Linn's forehead. Then Kiah smiles at me and repeats the kiss on my cheek. Evardo gets one too, but not her own double. The two of them just let their fingertips touch. Then my Kiah gently pushes the foreign one towards her companions.

The other Evardo waves to us. "You'd better get going," he says with a concerned glance at Linn, as always the practical one.

Linn is already struggling to breathe. Her skin has started to feel colder, even with the warmth it receives from me. My Kiah and Evardo position themselves on opposing sides of me and Linn. As they're about to take hold of us, I look towards Amira. She is covering her face with one hand, teardrops floating though her fingers.

"Evardo is right," she whispers. "You have to hurry."

Apparently, this is the farewell I get. It feels unbearable to leave her like this, not understanding why she sounds so bitter. But there's no time for questions. I need to concentrate on Linn, letting Kiah and Evardo lead us both away. Linn trembles, occasionally letting out a whimper. We have to hurry.

I hold Linn close while Kiah and Evardo cautiously ease us, first through the passageway and then across the living room. Only when we reach the entrance to the connecting passage do I glance up. Out of the corner of my eye, I notice a figure a couple of meters away. Amira has been following us.

"I'll wait for you here," she calls out. "Will you come back one last time, for my sake?"

My heart somersaults, and I hastily nod while Evardo and Kiah maneuver me and Linn's increasingly trembling body into the opening.

"If I can," I say, but I'm not sure if she hears me.

PERMANENCE

During the rest of our stay, Kiah spoke no more of her idea. Only when we had left the zoi and were on our way back to Earth in the space shuttle, did she present it to the rest of the crew, not as a question, but as another plan.

Once we had returned home, she would contact ETLEA's management, proposing that the next expedition would be of a permanent nature. If and when the next zoi appeared, the organization would launch the usual expedition of astronauts to establish themselves in its interior. But unlike earlier teams, these astronauts wouldn't leave towards the end of the usual orbiting time. Assuming the habitat formed as expected, and that this zoi too started providing the astronauts with air, food and water, they were to remain in it. When it broke out of its orbit around the sun, they would journey with it, out of the solar system.

For Kiah, the only question that remained, was who wanted to join. But some of our fellow crew members were fundamentally opposed the idea, and the subsequent discussion came to dominate the entire journey. Whenever we gathered, for work or for leisure, the topic would inevitably find its way into the conversation.

"Don't you realize how selfish it is?" Like the rest of us, the geneticist Yuze was strapped into a workstation in the space shuttle's lab, surrounded by wires, control panels and screens. We had managed to work in silence for about half an hour, but apparently, he could no longer keep his thoughts to himself. "You have already been on two missions, but instead of making room for others, you absolutely have to push things to a level we aren't ready for, just to ensure that you will be among the first to follow a zoi into space."

Kiah leaned out from the alcove she was seated in. "So, you'll just assume that they keep coming? Continue with time-limited stays in zoi after zoi, though each of them might be the last we ever see? We'll never be truly ready to make the leap. So we might as well do it at the next opportunity, while we hopefully have the chance."

"While *you* have the chance, you mean." Yuze angrily pounded his keyboard while he spoke. "The rest of us would be perfectly content with spending another year in the next zoi. Perhaps that limits what we can achieve, but there's still plenty to explore and experiment with."

"Not compared to what a permanent residence would give us."

"Of course not. And someday, we will get to that. When we have a better understanding of how the zois affect us. When we have become more adept at arranging ourselves within them, and when we understand the force that propels them through space. Then, we could learn to control that force, and thereby not just travel outward, but also back home. Until then, we are talking about a one-way ride away from Earth. Who, apart from you, would be willing to sign up for something like that?"

"I would," Linn calmly responded. "It's a unique opportunity, to become the first true space explorers. What could ever surpass that?"

"A life on our own planet!" Yuze gave up pretending to work. He freed himself from his chair and turned toward Kiah and Linn, freely floating in the narrow space between workstations. "I have family and friends back home. I have a whole world, filled with places I love and places I haven't visited yet. Why would I abandon all that in order to spend the rest of my life enclosed within a creature we know practically nothing about? It may be heading for interstellar space, but it could be centuries before it reaches another star. We will be long dead."

"Maybe we will." Kiah had turned as well, though she remained in her seat. "And maybe we won't. You of all people ought to recognize the implications of the epigenetic alterations apparent in our own organisms."

"And I of all people know how little we understand the consequences! Our aging process seems to be put on hold, but this could have all kinds of side effects, and we can't be sure if it's a lasting phenomenon. Even if it is, is that something to desire? We have just spent a year in a zoi. It has certainly been interesting, and I would happily do the same thing again. But living like that for centuries, perhaps even millennia? Thanks, but no thanks! I have no desire for that."

"Some of us do," Kiah said, looking around at the rest of us.

I met her gaze but said nothing. Sipho and a couple of the others shook their heads. Evardo followed the conversation but showed no sign of his thoughts. Marina was the only one to reply.

"I'm not sure. Maybe. All my life, I have been studying the cosmos, and traveling beyond the solar system, perhaps even reaching another star—that would be incredible. But is it worth the price?"

"Yes, it is," Kiah asserted. "The zois represent an opportunity to reach the universe and understand the basic nature of life, which we may only have for a limited time. Of course, it's still possible that someone else will be able to exploit it in a decade or two, but what really prevents us from doing it now? All we're putting at stake is our own lives. And those lives will probably be prolonged rather than shortened."

Yuze crossed his arms in front of his floating body. "You have no idea what will happen to you during that journey. We have a vague notion of why the zois strive to incorporate foreign organisms, but it's mere speculation. The moment you're out of orbit, their hospitality might veer into something entirely different. Besides, the fact that the zois are altering our biological systems is frightening in itself, even if those alterations seem to be benign."

Linn regarded Yuze with something resembling contempt. "I'm not afraid of being changed," she said. "Whatever the zoi does to me, I will endure it. Sooner or later, we will learn how to take control of the process, to shape ourselves, like we're shaping the zoi substances into useful materials. Even in the interstellar vacuum we will be on a voyage of discovery, into the zoi and into ourselves."

Who did I agree with? I had mourned leaving the zoi without knowing if I would ever encounter another one. Compared to last time, we had made some progress, but not that much. There were limits to how much we could achieve within a single year, precisely because we had to start over each time. A permanent residence would open up entirely new opportunities to make ourselves at home within the zoi and truly get to know it. In that sense, I was on the same page as Kiah and Linn. At the same time, I agreed with Yuze that Kiah was rushing things. We still had a completely insufficient understanding of the processes altering fundamental parts of our physique.

Then again, every change so far had been beneficial, or even necessary. The discomfort we experienced in the beginning was only a transitional phase we had to get through, allowing the zoi to adjust the way in which our bodies responded to weightlessness. Halting the aging process would allow us to be part of a centuries-long journey. That the zoi also seemed to inhibit our reproductive system might conceivably be considered a different matter. I hadn't had a single period during my stays within the zoi, and no sexual urges either. But how much of a sacrifice would that really be? I didn't want children anyway, and ever since my breakup with Natan, the very idea of having sex with anyone had seemed daunting.

Yuze raised his hands. "Fine. If you're really that crazy, I won't stand in your way! We'll see what ETLEA has to say about your proposal."

ETLEA said exactly what was expected: management would consider the possibility, but any decision would have to await a thorough examination and evaluation of all data obtained from the newly completed expedition, a process which would take years. Though they appreciated our ardor, they wouldn't send us on a suicide mission.

Personally, I wavered between determination and doubt. Although I endorsed Kiah's proposal, along with Linn and Marina, I wasn't certain if I would be willing to leave Earth for good. It might be a journey into the Galaxy, but it came with considerable limitations. I would be tethered to the zoi, and it would be an overwhelmingly long time before it reached another solar system.

In the latter half of our recent stay, we had worked on integrating a number of technological objects into the alien organism, including a telescope which, after numerous failed attempts, we had finally managed to incorporate into the outer surface. Hopefully, the same thing would be possible in the next zoi. But neither the telescope nor any other appliance would stay functional forever.

Fabricating equipment able to withstand the zoi environment for even a year was difficult enough. Besides, we had to consider the risk that at some point the zoi would categorize all our effects as dead weight and destroy them. Since we departed from our latest host, the usual thing had happened. After a while, the devices we had left behind ceased to function. So far, this hadn't happened while humans were still present, but we had no way of knowing how it would work out on a longer time scale.

Linn believed she would be able to manufacture spare parts for the electronics out of zoi material, but this was just speculation. We could easily end up without any technological aids, including the telescope and communication equipment. Though we might still survive, we would then be utterly confined. It would have no significance at all where in the universe we found ourselves. The zoi would constitute our entire world.

The only sensible thing would be to wait. First, we had to become more familiar with the zois; to gather experience and develop solutions. And like Yuze said, we ought to make room for other people. On future zoi expeditions other crews would collect new data, and by doing research on that data, we could maintain our personal connection to the zois, at least in a theoretical sense.

But then I would talk to Kiah and get caught up in her burning enthusiasm. Like her, I had dedicated my life to the zois. How could I let this opportunity slip away?

A year passed after our return, then two. ETLEA was preparing the next expedition, but it remained undecided on who would participate and what the nature of it would be—another time-limited stay, or the voyage of exploration that Kiah wanted out into space and into the zoi. She was pushing for a decision, and I supported her, even though I was still in doubt.

Slowly, things advanced. ETLEA's management talked about making room for both possibilities. When the usual time had passed, some participants would remain in the zoi, while others left. Those who had opted to stay would be able to change their mind until the moment their fellow crew members fired up the space shuttle to begin their journey home.

Kiah wasn't entirely satisfied. She would have preferred the goal to be unambiguous, though she understood that this was probably the best we could hope for. She was terribly disappointed when Marina backed out, and we were both equally astonished when Evardo signed up in her place. I suspected he did it more for our sake than his own, but he seemed as determined as the rest of us.

Then a zoi made its appearance in the sky, only three years after the departure of its predecessor. The way was now clear. If I chose to pursue it.

PARTING

When we move back through the connecting passage, I notice that it has grown longer. The membrane walls appear thinner; stretched, and possibly on the verge of eroding away. We're returning to our own habitat at the last minute.

I keep Linn close to my own body, attempting to provide her with warmth and strength. Her limbs feel cold and feeble, except when her muscles contract in sporadic spasms. Even the spasms are gradually weakening, just like her breathing and heartbeat.

Finally, we arrive. Kiah pushes Linn and me through the entrance to the chamber, still clutched in a tight embrace. Even when we're inside, I dare not let go. Only when we have reached the soft, bumpy wall do I begin to loosen my grip. I turn to detach one side of Linn from myself and gently push her into the membrane whose tongues and threads are reaching for her. I'm not frightened by them anymore. They are the only thing that can keep Linn alive.

They're doing their job. The moment she's settled, her back and hips half buried and her entire body partially enveloped by the caressing threads, her skin starts regaining its warmth and color. Her breathing eases. She inhales deeply, lets out the air in a sigh, and smiles.

"It's good to be home," she whispers.

It's true, we're home, all four of us. A deep contentment spreads from Linn's smile to my insides, prompted by my relief that the transplanting proved successful. Probably also by hormonal influence from the zoi, but even that doesn't worry me. Everything is as it should be.

Except for one detail: I promised Amira to come back and say goodbye.

It's probably too late. My body tells me to forget all about it, but that's exactly why I have to try. If I simply give up in advance, if I don't even make an attempt to return to my other self for a farewell, then my humanity and whatever remains of my free will is already lost.

Kiah and Evardo aren't exactly pleased to hear what I have in mind, but they don't try to talk me out of it. Neither of them accompanies me. They have said their goodbyes.

The entrance to the connecting passage is almost gone. The hole has closed up, leaving a spot with a slightly different color and texture than the rest of the wall. A penetrable area. I can still go through if I want to, but where will it lead me?

Through the semi-transparent walls of the living room, I try to ascertain if the passage is still there. A drawn-out structure can still be discerned, but it appears frayed, and in several places, the walls have collapsed. Moving through it is out of the question. Still, I try pushing my hand though the spot on the wall. If I sense cytosol on the other side, I will know that any possibility of returning to Amira has been lost. Even if the zoi has copied the spacesuits, they probably won't be functional. Not everything in them is organic.

My hand encounters a slight resistance from the penetrable membrane. Then I feel liquid; not the cytosol, but a thinner kind, like in Kiah's aquarium. The fluid that I know I may someday have to breathe instead of air, though I have tried my best to suppress that knowledge.

My chest tightens, as if my lungs are already grappling with the unfamiliar sensation. I remember Kiah effortlessly breathing the liquid, even speaking within it. I ought to be able to do the same. In theory. The mere notion makes me nauseous. Suddenly, even the air seems too dense for my lungs. I will never be able to do it. Anyway, it would be futile, because Amira would feel the same. If I can't manage to go out there, she can't either.

On the other hand: If I can do it, so can she.

Why didn't we just say goodbye while we had the chance, like everyone else, when we fetched Linn? Perhaps because our relationship is a little more complicated than those between the other twins. Amira is evidently bitter about something, and it will take more than a smile and a touch to reach the point where we can part as friends,

My thoughts stray to the communication equipment. As far as I know, none of us has used it since the shadows first appeared. Personally, I couldn't bear facing the life and the world I have left behind. Now I'm not sure if we will ever be able to resume contact, with Earth or with our twins. We may never get the copied equipment to work, and even if we do, I will probably feel the same way about Amira as I do about Natan. No electronically transmitted message will be able to change the fact that I have left her for good. We will never meet again.

What if Amira is already out there in the liquid? Maybe she's struggling to breathe while she's waiting for me to take the plunge. Then I'm the only one being a coward, failing once more. I simply have to do it.

My hand is still stuck in the wall. I pull back my arm slightly, feeling for a solid edge. There's nothing to kick off from, so I must pull myself through. The material gradually solidifies, and eventually, I get a grip. Not leaving myself any time to think or take one last breath of air, I move forward in a jerk.

The soft material of the opening glides against my face, over my shoulders, and the rest of my body. Then it's replaced by liquid stroking my skin, soft as a warm breeze. It feels almost like air, to my open eyes as well. But only almost. Moving my arm, I meet some resistance. This *is* liquid, and I feel far from certain that I will be able to breathe it. Last time, even though I watched Kiah breathing and heard her speak, I couldn't bring myself to follow her example. This time I'm on my own, with no example to follow, no one to help me if things go wrong.

I wait until my body is screaming for oxygen. Then I inhale.

My lungs fill with something much too thick and viscous. My vision darkens. In a moment I will be dead, suffocated—but it doesn't happen. I remain conscious. What's making me feel dizzy and sick is simply fear, and this fear gradually lessens. I release the liquid through my nose and mouth and inhale once more, trying not to think, just let the liquid flow in and out, as if it were air, as if everything were normal.

I take a look around. The area containing the thin

liquid has no clear boundary against the cytosol but seems to transition gradually into it. The organelles circumvent the area. They too prefer to avoid the unfamiliar medium.

Where is Amira? If she's waiting for me somewhere, it's not here. I suppose she hasn't dared to enter the fluid after all. My gaze follows the last remnants of the connecting passage, which is in the process of disintegrating. A little further along, there is a spot where the fragments are moving in opposite directions. As if an invisible barrier has emerged, split up the passage and started pushing the two parts away from each other.

On the other side of the boundary, I catch sight of her. She's far away, but she's approaching, and I do the same, swimming forward through the liquid with clumsy strokes, tentatively, because the element I transverse isn't water, but something thinner and lighter. I'm swimming against a current. It's not that strong, but if I stop moving for a moment, I slowly drift backwards, away from Amira.

Something presses in from both sides toward the barrier between us. I concentrate on making my swimming motions more forceful and efficient. For a while, I don't look up. When I do, Amira's face is right in front of me.

We both halt and immediately start drifting backwards. I kick forward again and reach out for her, all reservations forgotten. But there's a certain point

I'm unable to pass, and she is on the other side. When she opens her mouth to speak, I only hear some muffled sounds.

"Amira!" I cry out, and immediately start coughing. Breathing is one thing, but speaking in the liquid is a deeply bizarre sensation. Another wave of fear threatens to overpower me, but I keep it under control and keep swimming to stay in place. We don't have long.

"Are you... okay?" The words seem to come from far away, even though Amira can't be farther from me than one meter. The barrier between us is dampening the sound.

"Yes. I just need to... adjust to this."

"How about Linn?"

"She made it. Being moved. She's back in the wall."

Amira's face twists. "You took her from us. The other one isn't Linn. Not anymore."

I understand her bitterness. Seeing the little, shrunken Linn together with her twin was unsettling enough. Now she's all Amira has left.

"The same will happen to our Linn. She'll also become part of the zoi."

"Yes, but right now you're still able to talk to her. I'm not."

"I'm truly sorry," I say, hoping she will know that I'm sincere. "But she made her own decision."

I'm getting used to speaking. This seems to go for

Amira too, but the sound of her voice is getting fainter. The physical distance between us is increasing, and the transparent material through which we are watching each other is being replaced by something else.

"You're right. She did." Amira closes her eyes for a moment. When she opens them again, her gaze flickers to both sides. "Amira, I think the zoi is dividing right now!"

Of course. What's approaching from all sides is the outer shell of the zoi. Soon, it will completely encase both of us, separating us forever.

"Can you forgive me?" I'm shouting, as I was barely able to make out her last words.

"Yes. If you can forgive me," she shouts back. "It has been difficult sometimes, for us both."

The window between us is rapidly shrinking. In a moment, she'll be gone.

"We had good times, too. I'll miss you, Amira."

I can't hear her response. Her face is the last thing I see.

Then the shell closes, and I'm alone.

HOME

The floor of the house gently rocked beneath me. I sat in the opening that faced the ocean, listening to Karim rummaging around in the kitchen. My visit had lasted four days, and I had seen what was left to see of Tabiteuea, the atoll in the island state Kiribati where Karim resided.

He emerged with a cup of coffee for both of us. As he sat down beside me, I noticed the multitude of grey hairs mixing in with the dark ones. He had turned fifty last year.

"Has anyone told you what Tabiteuea means?" he asked.

"Several times," I replied. "The land without chiefs. They take great pride in that."

"They do." We sat in silence for a while. A fishing boat sailed by, and Karim waved to the people on board. "There's not much land left," he continued.

"But they don't let that discourage them. The land was never the most important thing here. It's the lagoon."

Even before the sea levels began to rise, Tabiteuea only stood a few meters above the surface, and presently the atoll was partly submerged. Mangrove thickets held together the last remnants of partly drowned land strips, where trees and bushes appeared to grow right out of the water. Villages and houses had been destroyed time and again during the past half-century, and although raising the buildings on stilts helped somewhat, in the long run it wasn't enough.

Most of the population had long since left the atoll, but the few who chose to stay had found another solution: letting the villages float on water. Residents drove piles into the lagoon floor, anchoring their house boats to them via flexible moorings. This way, the village could adapt to the drastic shifts in sea levels, and though the ever more frequent tropical storms were still a threat, they caused much less havoc than they used to.

Karim had come to take part in the effort to protect the coral reefs, which were far more significant than the land. These reefs needed optimal growth conditions to keep pace with the rising sea. Otherwise, the whole atoll would eventually disappear.

"Karim?" I said his name without quite knowing

what I wanted to ask. When he looked at me, I continued. "Are you... content with your life, or do you sometimes regret not having settled down? Never starting a family?"

"I live my life the way I want to live it," he said with conviction. "People kept telling me this would change as I got older, but it never did. If I ever settle down, it will be because I'm forced by age or illness."

"So, you don't miss having a home?"

"I do have a home. This entire planet." Karim extended a hand towards the water. "The Pacific flows into the other oceans, and this all-encompassing sea connects every island and continent. The air that I'm breathing right now might have passed by our childhood home at some point. That's enough for me. I feel at home everywhere."

"But you wouldn't in space."

"I wouldn't. But maybe you will."

I took a deep breath. "Yes, maybe. But the decision can't be undone. If I leave with Kiah and the others, I can never return to Earth."

"And if you stay here, you will never follow a zoi into space. The two options are mutually exclusive. You simply have to choose."

Simply. I inhaled once more, taking in the scents of the sea and the corals, the light breeze against my skin. There was so much I would never again experience if I left. But no human had yet ventured beyond the solar system. And no human had truly come to understand the zois.

Karim wrapped an arm around me, and I leaned against his shoulder.

"Little Amira," he said. "My niece who has become a full-fledged astronaut and xenobiologist. You have achieved so much already, no matter which choice you make."

"But sometimes I still feel like a child," I murmured. "The child who sat with you and witnessed the first encounters with the zois. Back then, everything was so simple, precisely because all I had was dreams for the future. Now these dreams have become reality."

"It's always scary when dreams come true, and being the first to step into unknown territory is both scary and dangerous. I won't encourage you to leave, but I won't try to talk you out of it either."

"What would you do if you were me?"

Karim shook his head. "I'm not you. We resemble each other in some ways, but not all. You are much more focused than I ever was."

"And because of that, you think I will choose differently." I sat up and pulled away from him. "Is that what you mean?"

"That's why I can't advise you. I hate it myself when others presume to know how I should live my life."

I thought about the many times Karim had resisted family pressure. How they reproached him for not getting a proper education and a steady job; for fooling around all over the world with no purpose or direction. But he had his own kind of purpose, that of helping others while seeing the world. Learning new skills and passing them on.

"I wish I weren't that focused," I say. "Perhaps that's my real problem, that I only have room for the zois in my life. I have pushed away even Natan, precisely because of that single-mindedness."

"You haven't completely pushed him away, have you? As I understand it, you remain friends."

"Yes, I visited him shortly before coming here. They have two children now, and a third on the way. He has an utterly amazing garden with biotopes suited for virtually every edible plant that exists, as well as the ones that are beautiful or simply interesting. To him, his family, their house and his garden are the center of everything. It's delightful to visit him and sense how happy he is."

My mind went back to the last evening at Natan's place. We sat between grapevines, fig shrubs, and peach trees, enjoying an almost entirely home-produced dinner. Their eldest child, Dale, who was now five years old, was playing with a crowd of neighboring kids, while the two-year-old, Nikki, toddled to and fro. Robin was seven months pregnant, with a belly that she herself claimed was bigger than Isabel's ever got, even with her second child. She loudly and cheerfully complained about how much she hated being pregnant, and how unfair it was that Isabel had felt splendid all the way through.

Coby talked about their latest art project, but was interrupted by a howl from Nikki, who had hurt herself and was now calling for the parent she usually sought comfort from. Coby had pulled the heaviest weight in looking after Nikki, and they were still the one who stepped in if she was sick or needed a break from the nursery group she usually went to. All six members of the family, children and parents, were very attached to each other, but some of them still had a special bond. The smile that Natan sent Coby when they returned, carrying Nikki, made me wonder if the two of them had become something more than co-parents. Natan hadn't said say anything about it, but I wasn't sure if he would have.

"So you don't regret letting him go? Karim asked.

I shook my head. "It was the right decision for both of us."

My happiness for Natan may have carried a hint of sadness, but no regret. I appreciated being a guest in his world, but I wouldn't have felt at home in it.

"In a way, that decision was just as significant," Karim pointed out. "You made it, and you chose right. You'll do the same this time."

"Let's hope so."

I gazed out over the seemingly endless sea. Back in the day, venturing out into the Pacific had been akin to going into space. The inhabitants of the archipelagos had developed extremely advanced navigation techniques, but if anyone happened to veer off course on their way to another island or atoll, they would still be doomed. The ocean was so vast that their chance of reaching land before starving to death was practically nonexistent.

In the zoi, we wouldn't starve to death. It seemed to hold an unlimited supply of food and water, not to mention air. But when it came to the journey itself, we were in much the same situation as seafarers of the past who set out from the coasts of New Zealand or South America without knowing their destination. They couldn't expect to find anything but the sea. Such a voyage should only be embarked upon if the journey was an end in itself.

"Is something wrong, Amira?"

Karim's voice sounded as if it came from afar. I blinked, slowly turning towards him.

"I'm fine," I said with a smile, and I meant it. For the first time in a very long while I felt completely at ease. I wasn't yet ready to put my decision into words. Like the house I was in, it was at the same time anchored and floating. But I had made it. I had chosen the journey.

CONSCIOUSNESS

For a while, I'm unable to move. The current sending me backwards has ceased, so I keep hanging there, in front of the spot where Amira just disappeared. I suspect that I'm crying, but my tears dissolve into the liquid.

Something touches my back. Probably some stupid organelle that has after all made its way into the new medium. I'm too numb to be startled, can't be bothered to turn around. But the touch persists. Eventually, I turn my head.

It's Kiah. She reaches for me, and suddenly I give no damn whatsoever about all the things that have kept us apart—her rapid change and adaption, my own fear mixed with something that, truth be told, was probably envy. I desperately need the comfort she offers. Gratefully, I let myself fall into her embrace, clutch her to me, and feel her strong arms hug back.

"Come inside, Amira," she says, her voice distorted by the liquid.

"Why?" I ask. "You must be used to this, and I have to get used to it too."

"Perhaps. But not right now."

No. Not right now. Right now, I need all the familiarity I can get. I start choking again. I know I can't afford to panic, that I must simply breathe the liquid in and out, calmly and composedly, like I have managed to do for quite a while, without any trouble. But I can't keep calm any longer. I heave the liquid in, cough it out. My lungs have had enough of it. They want air.

Something is pulling me away.

"We're almost there. Just a moment longer."

It's Kiah murmuring to me. A substance firmer than the liquid slides against my face and shoulders, and the next time I cough, the fluid comes out in bubbles. I'm surrounded by air. With gurgling breaths, I gasp for it; coughing violently, over and over, but I can't get all the fluid out. I start to vomit, and Kiah pushes yellow, foul-smelling chunks away while she holds me, instructing me to breathe deeply, in and out. Slowly, I calm down. I accept the clicking sounds from my lungs, the way that the liquid keeps flowing out with every exhalation. It's okay. It will pass.

"Amira?" It's Evardo's voice now, controlled to a degree which suggests that he is very concerned. "Amira, can you tell me what happened?"

"She's gone," I sob. "They all are." I recount my last sight of my twin; how the cell wall closed around her.

"Then the division is concluded." Evardo sounds relieved. "I understand your grief, Amira—but this is how it had to be. And we should be grateful that it went well."

I hadn't even considered the other option. That something in the division process might have gone wrong, with fatal results for us, as well as for the zoi. We're surrounded by empty space, protected only by the shell I was so heartbroken to see close off around me. I ought to consider myself extremely fortunate that it did.

"Will the same thing happen again?" I whisper. "Another cell division? New copies of us?"

"It will," Kiah replies. "Perhaps not until our next visit to a star, but it's possible that the zoi has gathered enough matter and energy for more than one division. In that case, it could happen soon."

She watches me while she speaks, evidently worried how I will react. I try to imagine what it will be like to go through the whole thing again. Having the shadow grow at my side, suddenly waking up as two versions of the same person, first inseparable and then repelled from each other. I can hardly bear the last thought, of yet another separation like the one I just endured. But I'm surprisingly okay with the rest of it. In a way, I can almost look forward to it.

"Oh well," I say. "Next time, we will at least understand what's happening ."

The worry in Kiah's face is replaced by a wide smile. She embraces me again, not gently and considerate this time, but tightly. Something akin to a whimper escapes her. Is she crying? Kiah never cries. But when she lets go of me, I see teardrops in the air between us.

"I'm so happy you take it that way. I've been afraid that you'd just give up."

I nod silently. If Kiah hadn't retrieved me just now, out in the fluid, I'm not sure if I would have found my way back. But she did come out for me, because she cares about me. She has cared for me the entire time, even when I thought she didn't. It was me who kept her at arm's length, because she was free from the fear that paralyzed me. It hasn't completely let go of me, but it has eased enough that I'm able to look forward.

Evardo floats towards us. "We'd better get back to Linn," he says. "She needs to know what happened."

Side by side, we head off; the three of us together, on our way to the fourth. It feels so right, and though I know the likely origin of that feeling, it doesn't make it any less genuine. Something has fallen into place. Even the awareness of what will eventually happen to Linn is no longer unbearable. As Kiah said, she will still be here. Her body and mind will be absorbed, but they won't disappear. She will be a part of the zoi. In a certain sense, the zoi will be her, perhaps more literally than I have so far been able to imagine.

As the first of us, I pass through the entrance to her chamber. This time, the sight of her doesn't fill me with horror and pity, but with love and gratitude. Her body is still fully visible, although the threads growing out of the wall are diligently working to encase and embed it. Soon she will start to shrink like her twin. But for a while longer, she will be this body, the human being Linn.

Her eyelids flutter. Kiah and Evardo join me, and we wait while she slowly wakes up.

"Amira." Linn has opened her eyes. She frees an arm and reaches out towards me. "Did you manage to say goodbye?"

"Yes," I reply as I float towards her. "I did."

"That's good." She furrows her brow. "I felt the division happen. It was a huge relief for the zoi. All of this has been hard on it. Like a difficult birth."

I know she is already closely connected to the zoi, but still—does she really sense its reactions?

"Then you know more than we do," Evardo says. "And here I thought we had to keep you informed because you are tied to this chamber. In reality, we are the ones who are confined, by being tied to our own bodies."

"That will change!" Kiah states. "We may not be able to transcend them as easily as you, Linn, but as we become more integrated..." With a glance at me, she cuts herself off. Apparently, that's how far she trusts my acceptance of the situation, and I have to admit that I'm struggling to embrace all the numerous perspectives which are suddenly opening up, each one more extreme than the other. But I must face the facts of what is going to happen to all of us, including me.

"We will become part of the zoi, mentally as well as physically." I sigh. "The idea still frightens me, but not as much as it once did."

Kiah's eyes light up. "Then perhaps you can see what it entails. Not just that the zoi will alter us. *It* will be changed by *us*, precisely because we are providing it with something it lacks: consciousness."

Of course. That realization follows naturally from what I already conceive about Linn and the zoi. But what will it mean in practice, for us and for it?

I turn towards Linn. "Do you agree that's how it will go?" I ask. "Or does the zoi already possess some kind of awareness that we just don't recognize? One we will be subordinate to?"

Linn closes her eyes once more. Her face is impassive, as pale as ever, and I'm not sure if she's breathing. Frantically, I reach for her hand. I should let her rest, but I'm not sure how long will we be able to communicate.

Eventually, she takes a deep breath. "No. It's not conscious in our sense of the word. It doesn't plan, doesn't make assessments. It exists, and it reacts. Automatically, but also... extremely elaborately. Its ability to make changes within itself, to influence us, is completely different from consciousness, but no less advanced." She frees her hand from mine, touching the delicate threads that move exploringly around her. "Finding my place within it isn't exactly easy, but I do have a place. The zoi creates it for me."

Is that reassuring? I'm not sure, but I must stop asking questions, as Linn is evidently exhausted. We should let her rest, even though this rest and the strength the zoi can provide comes at a price.

"I'll stay with her," Evardo says. "Why don't the two of you take a look around to see what we're missing and what isn't working? The sooner we know, the better."

"Good idea." Kiah waves at me. "Come on, Amira."

DEPARTURE

We gathered in the holoroom to watch the space shuttle take off. It had brought us to the zoi, and now it carried away the other half of the crew, back to Earth.

This is my last chance, I repeatedly told myself as they prepared for departure, as they filed out through the living airlocks, as they announced that they were now on board, that they were about to start the engines. Every moment, I expected to panic, to regret my decision at the last minute, or when it was too late.

Instead, I was filled with perfect tranquility. My decision couldn't be undone. We were here, and there was no turning back. Soon, we would be the ones to depart with the zoi.

I felt Kiah's hand in mine, smiled at her and met a bright gaze that had long since turned away from the rapidly diminishing dot representing the space shuttle. Then I turned to the other two. Linn was paler than usual, perhaps a bit tense. Evardo looked somewhat worried but seemed composed.

In that moment, it hit me that all three of them were essentially strangers, even Kiah who had been my friend for so long. At the end of the day, I knew very little about her, and even less about the others. Now they were my entire world, along with the zoi and the universe surrounding us.

This was a world I would have to learn to live in. I no longer had any choice.

OUTLOOK

On this survey, we take the time to thoroughly examine everything in the new habitat, testing what needs to be tested. Some things work, others don't. We're not lacking anything essential for our survival. Strictly speaking, all truly essential needs are covered by the zoi, but there are man-made objects and technology I would be very reluctant to do without.

It was always part of the premise for this journey that eventually all items we brought along with us would cease functioning. We had counted on being able to reproduce most of them through Linn's expertise, and we certainly hadn't expected to suddenly be left with copies, created by a being with no comprehension of earthly technology. Our twins have all the original equipment, which seems unfair. But we have a Linn that we can still talk to. I suppose there's a justice in that.

The holoroom is the last we go through. This is where all our most advanced technology is located. I try not to think about the possibility that nothing in there works, because of missing non-organic components that we're unable to replace, or because the replication wasn't accurate enough. Kiah activates the projector, and initially it seems to work, like it did in my own hasty test. But the holographic projections that subsequently appear have nothing to do with the usual interface. For a few seconds, we silently watch the seemingly random shapes and colors. Then Kiah clutches her head.

"Shit! Then it's just a superficial imitation. A colored lights-machine. That's all." She kicks the wall membrane of the holoroom, and the force of her own motion propels her backwards, into more devices affixed to the opposite wall. Luckily, they are all behind bioplast covers protecting both them and her from harm. "What are we supposed to do with that?" she shouts into the air. "Couldn't you have made a real fucking effort?"

"Kiah. Calm down." I grab her arm and pull her into the center of the room. "Why are you losing your temper? Just a few hours ago, you declared that we should learn how to manage without human technology."

"I was referring to the trinkets that Evardo talked about. Insignificant metal tools. This is completely different! Without the equipment in here, we'll be deaf, blind, and dumb."

"I remember us discussing that possibility, even before we left Earth. You knew that was a risk we would have to accept."

"Yes. In theory. But that it actually happened... We can't see the outside, can't communicate with anyone, and we lost all our data. No holofilms or VR to watch. No books to read or music to hear. No scientific facts to build on, no tools for analyzing them. All we have is what happens to be stored in our own memory, for as long as that lasts."

"Don't jump to conclusions." I turn towards the most meticulously sealed section of the holoroom equipment, the container storing our data units. The units are visible through the transparent surface, spread out in a branching coral-like structure composed of algae growths. "If there's one thing the zoi has copied accurately, it's probably this," I say. "Information in the shape of genetic material, that's something it ought to comprehend."

"But what's the use if we have no way of deciphering it? The zoi understands DNA, but it clearly has no conception of holographic technology. In a way it's even worse to know that it's all there, but we can't access it. Like space. We know it's right outside, but we can't see it."

Now I'm the one who has to make an exasperated Kiah accept the situation and think constructively.

Secretly, I feel more like conceding to her despair. Together, we could rage against the zoi, and perhaps against our twins who have everything we lack. It would certainly feel satisfying. But it won't do any good.

"We can't give up this easily. Maybe Linn will know how to solve it."

Kiah shakes her head in resignation. "If she could come in here and tinker, she might manage to work it out—but there's no way she'll be able to do that. I'm not sure whether she has the strength to even advise us."

Probably not. It's been a long time since Linn was able to work. If she forces herself to try, it will weaken her further, likely without achieving anything.

"Then the rest of us will have to look into it. If we give it a genuine try, we may be able to make sense of it, even though we're not exactly experts..." At the sight of Kiah's expression, I trail off. She's staring at the abstract, holographic shapes, as if they have transformed themselves before her eyes.

"Make sense of it," she repeats. "Perhaps it *does* make sense. Perhaps I can..." She starts touching some of the patterns. They visibly react to her touch, maybe not in the exact same way as the regular interface, but a response is a response. It can be interpreted, and that interpretation may lead to some kind of mutual understanding. Communication is Kiah's expertise. "Yes," she whispers. "I think it might work. But I need to concentrate. Fully."

She works frantically, muttering to herself while she manipulates the holograms. It goes on for a long time, or at least I think so. My sense of time is slipping. My mind is whirling with speculations about a future that at this moment seems unbearably uncertain. Too many aspects of it are floating freely, in the air, in space, in the cytosol and in the breathable fluid which is our future. Then Kiah cries out in triumph.

"I did it! I have a connection to something in the outside surface. Either the telescope or the zoi's own sensory apparatus."

The room darkens, I'm not sure how. No black balloon has unfolded, like the one that in the original projection equipment would shield us from the bioluminescence. The zoi must be doing it. Another need it has detected and proceeded to fulfill, perhaps in connection with its reading of the technology we have incorporated into it, which it has now reproduced in a version of its own.

As the darkness descends, the stars light up around us. I have never seen so many, never had such a lucid vision of space, not even with the best instruments in ETLEA's possession. It's as if I'm not only seeing it, but feeling it, using some kind of sensory faculty that I have no name for. The zoi's sense of the universe.

A slight touch to my skin alerts me to Kiah's

presence right beside me.

"Do you feel it too?" she asks.

"Yes," I whisper. "'But it's so... strange." I clutch my head, overwhelmed by the sight and the unfamiliar sensations. "*Everything* is strange, and it will only get worse. Will we ever get used to it?"

"With time, we will. And we have plenty of time. The rest of eternity. At least in principle."

"Eternity?" I turn towards Kiah, but her figure blurs in my vision. My eyes tremble, unable to readjust from the astronomical distances to looking at something so close. I squint and lift a hand to cover my gaze. "Do you mean that the zoi will make us... immortal? We know that it slows our aging process. But that must have its limits."

"You're a biologist, Amira. You know what happens to the age of a cell when it divides. Wait—I'm trying to tone down the projection a bit. You can look up now."

I remove my hand, blinking to clear my vision. In front of us, I see some colored strings, twisting and twining among each other in rotating motions while Kiah's fingers play with them. I'm now able to get a focus on her. The stars are still there, but they've faded into the background.

"The age of a cell." I ponder the issue for a while. "When cell division has been completed, the original cell no longer exists. It has been replaced by two daughter cells, both of them equally newborn."

"Exactly! So what are we right now?"

My mouth gapes, I'm not sure for how long. "That's not the same thing," I eventually manage to exclaim. "We're still the same people. Even if the zoi created copies of us."

"Not copies," Kiah states. "I was the first to use that word, but I was mistaken. The zoi transformed one person into two, impossible to tell apart, both convinced that they were the original. And they were, to the same extent, both right and wrong."

I shake my head. Through all of this, I have held on to my conviction of being the authentic Amira, though for the sake of peace, I have let the subject drop.

"One of us *has* to be the original. Until it woke up, the other was only a shadow. We just don't know who's who."

"Up at certain point, that was probably true. But the shadow was physically connected to the body, and the two flowed into each other, the shadow drawing biological and genetic material from the body, while both formed new tissue based on what was already there. If any difference remains, it is essentially meaningless. We have been created anew, as two specimens."

There should be lots of counterarguments, but they get stuck in my throat. Deep down, I know Kiah is right. I look down at myself. A human body. Muscle, skin, bones and organs. How much was created by the zoi?

"So, you think this will make us live forever?" I ask. "Being renewed by an endless series of cell divisions?"

Kiah nods. "As long as the stars still shine, and we are able to travel from one star to another, collecting energy. Ultimately, the law of entropy may extinguish the last of them, or another cosmological event will terminate our journey, once and for all. But that's so inconceivably far into the future that in effect, it's still an eternity."

"But every division will create two versions of us, and some of them will perish. Space is a dangerous place." It still surrounds us, the cosmic void, punctuated by infinitely distant flecks of starlight. No, not infinitely distant. If we essentially have eternity at our disposal, they have come within reach. Visiting star after star is a viable prospect.

"Most of us will probably perish at some point," Kiah concedes. "But as long as a single unit makes it to the next cell division, we will still exist."

"*We* won't. Something that used to be us will exist as a part of some future being, mutated beyond recognition."

"By then, it will be us! We will truly be spacefarers, adapted to a space-borne existence, as the zois always were, but also capable of choosing our own course, of making decisions and responding deliberately to everything we encounter on our journey."

I still see the stars around me, but also the zoi. The wall membrane and the life form it represents are gradually more visible through the holographic projection. Both are my reality and my future. I will live here, within the zoi, perhaps forever. Gradually, the distinction between me and it will vanish. Together with Kiah, Evardo, and in some sense also Linn, I will *be* the zoi, its consciousness and will.

"It still scares me," I say. "Especially this immensity of *time*. Not just eternity, but the time it will take us to get from one sun to another. Centuries of traveling through nothingness. Perhaps there's a reason why the zois aren't conscious. It would be unbearable."

Kiah stretches out her arms towards the stars around us. Her long, frizzy hair billows around her face while she gazes out, into eternity. "This immensity of time," she repeats, then falls silent for a while, floating in the midst of the universe, before she continues. "Our relationship with time will have to evolve, but this evolution will in itself take time. A time we'll need to fill."

"Do you think we will be able to make it work properly?" I nod towards the cases containing the electronics. "Will you be able to connect the projector to the data units and the communication equipment?"

Kiah responds to my question by moving her

fingers in the air. This triggers a new projection of holographic shapes swirling before our eyes. Some of them proceed out into the room, toward the various devices. Even though Kiah's gaze is fixed on the threads, it seems distant. Once again, I have the staggering feeling of a new sense unfolding. Right now, it's just passively present, like when you gaze into the dark or listen to the silence. But it's there.

"I'm not sure. Establishing a connection to the surroundings was relatively simple. It encompasses a kind of input that the zoi is familiar with. The rest of it I will have to work on. Probably for some time."

She moves towards the container holding the data-storing algae, conjuring up new holograms, with threads reaching for the transparent cover. Behind it, the algae start glowing faintly. I hold my breath while a single spark travels over the coral structure, fluctuating in hue and intensity as it moves. Then Kiah withdraws her hand, and the holograms disappear.

"I have established a connection, but we'll have to proceed with caution. To the zoi, this is simply genetic material, and I'm afraid it will approach it the wrong way."

I hadn't thought of that. What if the zoi considers the algae to be just another life form to integrate and modify?

"Could it dissolve the container?" I ask.

"Easily. I have tried to communicate that it

should leave it untouched, that the algae are tremendously important in their present shape, to us as well as to itself. I can only hope it understood."

"Communicate—how?"

"I hardly know." Kiah grimaces. "The holo-interface plays a part, but other kinds of exchange are involved too. Perhaps they could be likened to the neural signals passing between body and brain. That's sort of how I imagine it. But for now, it's very faint."

We observe the algae in silence. For a while longer, we will have to live with the contingency that we may never regain access to their content, just like we have no assurance that we'll ever be able to send and receive messages between us and other humans. At the moment, our new form of connection to the zoi remains too obscure to be of any use beyond what we have just done, looking outside.

We're able to sense the world around us. That makes us travelers rather that prisoners.

METAMORPHOSIS

So little is left of her. A faint outline of her figure is all that remains visible in her old bedroom wall, now part of a larger room, a merging and subsequent expansion of Linn's chamber and the holoroom. It has replaced the old living room as our common lounge, allowing all four of us to be together. Back when Linn was still occasionally conscious, she told us she preferred it this way. Partly or fully asleep, she would listen to the sound of our voices and still feel like a part of the crew.

Constantly being reminded of her condition was distressing at first. But gradually, my grief reshaped itself, and in this moment, months since the last time I heard Linn's voice and met her gaze, I no longer know how to name the feeling induced by looking at her. These last remains of a human body, are they still her in any meaningful way? Sometimes, I believe I sense her presence in an entirely different form, as a shift in the abstract and indefinite connection between us and the zoi.

"Are you ready?"

It's Evardo's voice. I turn to see him floating towards me from the entrance to the room. Kiah is still guarding it, her hands smoothing out the holes in the membrane which is becoming increasingly porous. We're still able to keep it sealed, but not for much longer.

"No." For what's unnervingly close to being the last time, the word leaves my mouth in aerial form. "I could never be ready for this, no matter how long I had to prepare."

We have postponed it for as long as we possibly could. Even Kiah is unsettled by the fact that this will be our final farewell to breathable air. Besides, we're not sure how a permanent immersion in liquid will impact our technological equipment. Hopefully not much. This tech is the zoi's own creation. So far, we've only managed to establish very limited functionality, and though we assume that the zoi would naturally have made it liquid-adapted, we can't be sure.

"I'm doing what I can," Kiah asserts. "But I keep getting less and less to work with."

A large bubble slips past her hand. Hastily, she seals the hole, but that only makes another one form.

"It's all right," I say. "Just let go."

Evardo's hand grasps mine. I clutch it tightly,

extending my other hand towards Kiah. She takes off from the wall membrane surrounding the opening. This, too, is starting to dwindle, yielding to the pressure of her feet without the usual bounce, though still firm enough to propel her towards us. Taking my hand, she simultaneously reaches out for the outline of Linn's arm. We'll face this together, all of us.

A few more bubbles escape the opening, drifting into the room. Then the entire surface bulges in towards us, not breaking free of the surrounding membrane, but rather absorbing it as the material dissolves into the liquid. The whole process seems incredibly slow, but my sense of time may be warped. My breathing follows a conspicuously drawn-out pace, considering what's happening around me. Perhaps the zoi is meddling with my hormonal balance, dilating time and inducing a sense of calm. Perhaps this is just a natural serenity, unexpected, but still my own.

Slowly and steadily, I inhale and exhale. The air fills my lungs and leaves them through my nostrils while the bulge of liquid closes in, getting hazy and dim as it expands. The air grows heavier, and with every breath it feels more and more like inhaling the liquid. By now, the sensation has become almost familiar, from the numerous times I have ventured into the pockets of breathable fluid. Staying there for a while is no longer an issue. But up to this point, all visits to it have been temporary. At any point, I could swim towards an opening into the habitat and pass through the membrane, back into the well-known medium of air. Now, the last residue of air is being transformed. Soon, it will no longer exist.

There's no specific moment in which one state gives way to the other. What I dreaded for so long has happened, and I don't feel the slightest hint of panic. All is well, and if that sensation originates from the zoi, it's fine by me.

The zoi is no longer foreign. It's my home, my world, in some sense, my body. I'm part of it, and it is part of me. In this moment, my self is genuinely merging with my host as well as my crewmates. We're connecting, through our hands, through the liquid, through impulses that might be called telepathic, if this word was applicable to the internal connections within the body. Right now, the unity encompassing us all is so powerful it almost engulfs all sense of being the single person, Amira. Something is thinking that name, but it seems to have lost its meaning. Does Amira exist at all, or is there only this new being, the human-zoi?

The answer flows in the liquid with everything else. But within this new, fluid sense of self there remains a few grains of a firmer substance, gradually rediscovering itself. One of the grains reestablishes a sense of identity, one that's tied to a distinct, physical entity. Two similar entities touch it. And a third...

"Linn?"

The sound of the name passes from my mouth

into the fluid, but the reply does not take an audible shape.

I am here, is the message, clear and unmistakable, though I can't say how it forms in my head. *I have been here all along.*

"Are you..." I hesitate for what amounts to several beats of the thing I once again recognize as my heart, "...only Linn, or are you also the zoi?"

Only-Linn no longer exists. But Linn exists as part of the zoi. I am both. As we all are.

For the first time in a while, I regard the bodies beside me. Evardo's. Kiah's. Turning my head a few additional degrees, I look at the remnants of the figure in the wall. Kiah lets go of it and releases my hand. Evardo detaches himself too. With gentle swimming movements, we all withdraw a bit from each other. We're more than sufficiently connected, even without physical touch.

"Are you all right?" Evardo's mouth shapes the words, and they resound in the liquid. "Has your new condition cured you?"

I am well. Linn's body no longer fights the environment. It has been integrated as a minor component of my full substance. Our body. The zoi.

"And do you now understand the zoi?" The slightly distorted sound of Kiah's voice has a ring of both eagerness and desperation. "Can you make it understand you?"

I/we have a growing understanding, of both human

and zoi. Much remains foreign to both sides. But I/we are learning.

The amalgamation of *I* and *we* resonates in my mind as a wordless concept. In all its elusiveness, it makes sense for the experience I just had. The boundaries to the self are shifting. For now, I have regained a sense of identity connected to this human body, but its demarcations remain somewhat blurred. A pure *I* no longer exists, since the temporary unification has left behind a fragment of *we*. It manifests in multiple forms: as an Amira/we corresponding to the self-identification of Linn's unity with the zoi, as a human/we representing the four of us, and as an all-encompassing human/zoi/we, which, in some sense, equals an I.

"Then help us," Kiah implores. "If you still have Linn's knowledge of BB-tech, and the zoi-part of you remembers how it recreated the tech-equipment, you should be able to make it function!"

Kiah has been struggling with the task ever since the division, for more than half an Earth year, but has only made progress in the shape of improved projections from the outside. The increasingly detailed holograms of space give us a rendering of the stars and other celestial objects around us, which is far more vivid than what purely human technology was ever able to provide. But when it comes to decoding the genetically stored data, we have made no headway at all. Similarly, we haven't picked up a single message from either Earth or our sister-zoi, and we haven't been able to transmit any messages ourselves.

Function? The unspoken thought expresses puzzlement. *Everything was accurately copied. All functions should be intact.*

"Perhaps. But space-projection is the only operative feature. The rest of them... I did my goddamned best, but I keep hitting a barrier of something I don't understand, or which doesn't understand me."

Evardo nods slowly.

"Linn, you must be able to recognize the problem, even though it's alien to the zoi." His liquid-borne voice sounds somewhat husky, but his articulation gradually improves as he speaks. "It has no concept of outward communication or deciphering of data not directly related to any physical substance in the immediate surroundings. This is a human need you must convey to it, if you can."

I'll try.

Does this reply come solely from Linn? The wordless thought *I* still contains a certain measure of *we*, the union of zoi and human—but the human element has become more prominent. I sense the exertion it takes. Linn's presence in the zoi is scattered and unfocused. Maintaining a human way of thinking can't be easy.

While we await her response, I observe the small

figure which used to be Linn. It appears unaffected by what's happening around it. Presumably, it's just an empty shell, like the remnants of a chrysalis. A pupating larva will dissolve itself, consuming and digesting its own body in order to build a new one. What has happened to Linn has some similarities to the pupal metamorphosis. The zoi has consumed and digested her, to unify with her body and mind. My own transformation is less radical, but it's still underway.

For a while, the Linn-zoi-entity remains quiet. Then a holographic projection forms around us, not showing space, but a Scandinavian forest of conifers and birches. This recording was among Linn's favorites. During the phase when the shadows grew, she and I spent quite a bit of time in that forest.

Kiah cries out in excitement. Evardo silently opens his mouth while reaching out for a branch. Of course, his hand passes right through it, like mine passes through the rock that I instinctively attempted to touch. This is just a projection, but it still makes a world of difference from being completely confined to the zoi environment.

If we are now able to access this recording, the same probably goes for the rest. Holofilm. Music. Literature. Scientific data. Everything.

I have found a way, is the content of the nonverbal message accompanying the projection. *The zoi/we have understood the exceptional nature of this genetic material.*

The projector will now be able to read and display it.

"Does the zoi know to leave the material unchanged?" Kiah asks. "If there's even the slightest risk that it will start to ingest or alter it, we will have to sever the connection."

I/we have encoded the rule that the genetic material must remain intact. This still allows the zoi/us to copy parts if it, in order to study and enhance them. One goal could be adding more senses to the footage, taken from your/our memories.

Someday, I may be able to feel the rock; to smell the pine needles and the moss. I ache for a variety of scents, and I hope it will be possible to sense them through the liquid. But one question remains.

"Can we communicate with the outside world?" I ask.

Communication is more intricate. In storage, messages correspond to all other data, but the processes of receiving or sending them are very different from projecting. We will await new incoming messages, learn how to intercept and decode them. Later, we will transmit our own.

"So, at some point, we will be able to contact Earth?"

I picture the holo from Natan that I watched the day before we discovered the shadows. In the time that followed, I couldn't deal with anything beyond my immediate circumstances, and after our separation from the other zoi, it was too late. I never managed to reply.

"Is Earth really the first thing on your mind?" Kiah asks. "This has a far wider perspective."

"Does it? To me, Earth didn't just cease to matter when we left it. Our friends and family haven't heard from us for more than half a year. We should let them know that we're still alive."

Kiah and Evardo exchange a glance, as if they share some understanding I ought to have too.

"Amira, they may not have heard from *us*," Evardo says. "But they almost certainly heard from our doubles in the other zoi. With the original equipment they shouldn't have any trouble exchanging messages with Earth."

The realization hits me like a blow. Natan isn't waiting for a sign of life from me, as he long since received such a sign from Amira. Unlike me, she has been able to respond to him, apologize for her prolonged silence and bring him up to speed on recent events. In the past months, they have probably exchanged several holos. Natan will be aware of my existence, but would he want to stay in touch with more than one version of his former girlfriend?

"I'm not saying we should forget about Earth." Some measure of empathy has entered Kiah's voice. "But it belongs to the past, and we already carry that past with us in the shape of the data storage. Now, it even sounds like the zoi will be able to animate the data to a whole different level than the holo projector can."

"So, what are the wider perspectives you mentioned?" I ask, though in this moment, I hardly care. "Something to do with the other zoi?"

"Not the other zoi, but *zois*, plural. Sooner or later, our host will divide once more, and over time we will become numerous. With no means of communication, each one of us will drift though space like a desolate creature, but if we can remain in contact, we will be part of a community."

"A community consisting of identical clones. More and more versions of ourselves." I try to imagine it. Not merely a single Other-Amira, but countless ones. Keeping in contact with them all does not just seem overwhelming, but futile.

"We won't stay identical," Kiah states with conviction. "From the moment we woke up in separate bodies, we already started developing different personalities. The Kiah and Amira aboard the other zoi aren't us."

"You speak of this Kiah and Amira as distinct individuals. But like us, they are in the process of losing that individuality."

"Yes, in a sense. But if anything, this makes contact even more important. What we are growing into, is an entirely new kind of being, not only adapted for living in space and traveling through it, but also intelligent and self-aware. Being able to interact will make a tremendous difference for those beings, despite the delays and constraints imposed by cosmic distances. And once we learn how to steer our journey, we will be able to meet up."

Kiah's gaze is no longer directed at me, but at the future vision she's depicting. "We could accompany each other on our travels," she continues. "We could settle somewhere, permanently, or for a while. We could establish new societies and cultures, even superorganisms. Somewhere in the galaxy, we may encounter other space-dwelling intelligences. Some of our zoi-kin may also have merged with conscious entities, or they may have become aware on their own accord. Not to speak of the entirely alien forms of life and consciousness which may be out there."

I picture it all, in a kaleidoscope of images with no distinct details, but infused with a vertigo of endless possibilities. Is this a shared vision conjured by Kiah's words? I glance at Evardo, and as our eyes meet, he gives a slight nod. He sees it too, and he knows what I'm thinking. We think it together, all of us, even Linn, in some sense even the zoi, though the zoi is doing its reflective thinking through us. Its age-old, purely instinct-driven system undertakes its own kind of reasoning, and in a glimpse, I am one with that reasoning. It only lasts a moment, as my human mind is not yet able to endure such a unity for longer durations. But someday, it will be.

A surge of joy emanates from the combination of Linn and the zoi. I see Kiah and Evardo smiling, and sense that I smile too while tears stream from my eyes, melding into the fluid around us. The future remains daunting and unfathomable. But whatever it entails, and however that will change me, it will be an astounding journey.

ACKNOWLEDGEMENTS

A lot of people have helped me writing this book, knowingly or not. The initial inspiration came from a Radiolab podcast dating back to 2016 called "Cellmates," about the endosymbiosis resulting in the formation of the complex cell. The very lively presentation of the concept made it settle in my mind and connect with other ideas before the basic vision for this book suddenly emerged, years later.

In the process of writing and revision, the other members of my writing group, Janne Hejgaard and Hugo Alrø, were an invaluable source of both critique and support. Without their comments and questions the story would have been a lot less interesting.

This is a work of science fiction, and I wanted my free speculation to be based in actual science. In this respect, I had invaluable help from biologist Simon Agner Holm and astrophysicist Brandon Tingley. Thanks for answering all my stupid questions and for catching some disastrous oversights that I will never admit to having made, should anyone ask.

Later on, Brandon did an equally invaluable job revising my translation of the text from Danish into English. Especially in the beginning, before I started to get the hang of it, this was somewhat of an undertaking. It made this book possible. I can never thank him enough.

I'm endlessly grateful to writer Seb Doubinsky for so many things that I hardly know where to begin. After reading another book of mine (in Danish), Seb encouraged me to try my luck in English. Along with Brandon, he has been a language consultant.

He helped me find a publisher. He keeps telling me that my stories are worth reading. He keeps buying me beer.

Thanks an awful lot to Spaceboy Books for accepting the manuscript. To William Brandon for a great collaboration on the edits. To Nate Ragolia for his enormous helpfulness and patience in all other respects, and for creating a stunning cover.

Last but not least, I thank Sifka for putting up with having a writer mom, and Johan for seemingly appreciating having a writer for a partner.

ABOUT THE AUTHOR

Jane Mondrup was born with a passion for weird and fanciful stories. Growing up in the small country Denmark in the 1980's she had limited access to Science Fiction and Fantasy books, so she read everything she could get her hands on. At some point she realized that writing your own stories was a lot like reading, but with the option—to some extend—of deciding what happened. She identifies as a nerd in all aspects of her personality. If there was a pronoun for nerd, she would use that.

ABOUT THE PUBLISHERS

Nate Ragolia is a lifelong lover of science fiction and its power to imagine worlds more hopeful and inclusive than the real one. His first book, *There You Feel Free*, was published by 1888's Black Hill Press in 2015. Spaceboy Books reissued it in 2021. He's also the author of *The Retroactivist* (2017). His most recent book, *One Person Can't Make a Difference* (2022), was featured on Tor.com's Can't Miss Indie Press Speculative Fiction list, and was translated into Italian for Ringworld Sci-Fi in 2023. He founded and edited *BONED*, a literary magazine, and also created two webcomics. Nate is also a husband and a dog dad.

Shaunn Grulkowski has been compared to Warren Ellis and Phillip K. Dick and was once described as what a baby conceived by Kurt Vonnegut and Margaret Atwood would turn out to be. He's at least the fifth best Slavic-Latino-American sci-fi writer in the Baltimore metro area. He's the author *Retcontinuum*, and the editor of *A Stalled Ox* and *The Goldfish* for 1888/ Black Hill Press.